JTB

Her thoughts were mired in confusion.

Whatever Joe felt when they were together, a part of it had to be the fact that her children helped to fill the void in his heart left by the loss of his own children. And how much of what *she* felt was due simply to her own need to have a man in her life again? Andrea didn't know.

"Can't we be honest with each other?" Joe wanted to kiss her so much that he could taste it.

"I'm not sure what the truth is," she murmured.

Reaching out, he touched her hair. "I want you."

She felt her knees tremble. "I know," she said steadily. "And I want you. But I've decided I can't have you."

She didn't look back as she climbed the steps and entered the house. Then the door closed and the porch light went out, leaving Joe alone in the night.

Dear Reader,

Sophisticated but sensitive, savvy yet unabashedly sentimental—that's today's woman, today's romance reader—you! And Silhouette Special Editions are written expressly to reward your quest for substantial, emotionally involving love stories.

So take a leisurely stroll under the cover's lavender arch into a garden of romantic delights. Pick and choose among titles if you must—we hope you'll soon equate all six Special Editions each month with consistently gratifying romantic reading.

Watch for sparkling new stories from your Silhouette favorites—Nora Roberts, Tracy Sinclair, Ginna Gray, Lindsay McKenna, Curtiss Ann Matlock, among others—along with some exciting newcomers to Silhouette, such as Karen Keast and Patricia Coughlin. Be on the lookout, too, for the new Silhouette Classics, a distinctive collection of bestselling Special Editions and Silhouette Intimate Moments now brought back to the stands—two each month—by popular demand.

On behalf of all the authors and editors of Special Editions,
Warmest wishes,

Leslie Kazanjian
Senior Editor

JEANNE STEPHENS
Neptune Summer

Silhouette Special Edition

Published by Silhouette Books New York

America's Publisher of Contemporary Romance

SILHOUETTE BOOKS
300 East 42nd St., New York, N.Y. 10017

Copyright © 1988 by Jeanne Stephens

ISBN: 0-373-09431-0

First Silhouette Books printing January 1988

America's Publisher of Contemporary Romance

Printed in the U.S.A.

JEANNE STEPHENS

loves to travel, but she's always glad to get home to Oklahoma. This incurable romantic and mother of three loves reading ("I'll read anything!" she says), needlework, photography, long walks during which she works out her latest books, and, of course, her own romantic hero: her husband.

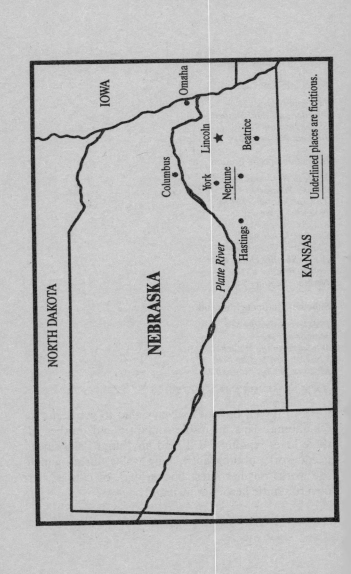

Chapter One

His eyes burned, and his shoulders ached from too many hours of close, detailed work. Joe tossed his pen aside and worked his neck and shoulder muscles to relieve the tension.

The desk was littered with overflowing ashtrays, dirty coffee cups, marketing plans and computer spread sheets. Colorful graphic displays of everything from sales projections to the latest fifty-two week trading range of National Motors common stock were strewn on the floor. Joe was used to clutter. His creative juices flowed more freely amid outward disorder. Having only recently recovered from a period during which the juices had dried up completely, he was superstitious about fiddling with the disarray.

His living quarters—a rented house on a quiet, shady street a mile from the plant—were neat and tidy, as though they were inhabited by a different man from the one who held sway in this big corner office. That was because nothing important happened there. Joe slept, showered and ate an occasional meal at the house, but he lived at the plant. He usually worked long after the rest of the office staff had gone home for the day.

He'd stopped trying to justify his workaholic habits to himself or others. He knew that his job had taken over his life, but it had also drowned his grief and loneliness. He considered it a satisfactory trade-off.

He leaned back in his chair, lit a cigarette, and noticed with surprise that the summer afternoon beyond the office windows was waning. Where had the day gone?

He vaguely remembered telling his secretary that he would be working on the new television promotion all afternoon and didn't want to be disturbed. Later, she'd opened the door to ask if he needed anything before she went home.

Taking a drag on the cigarette, he rolled his head slowly back and forth. He reached for the nearest cup, took a swallow of cold coffee, grimaced and set the cup down. He was as hungry as a bear coming out of hibernation. Had he eaten lunch? He couldn't remember.

He stubbed out his cigarette and went into his private bathroom, which was separated from his office by a short hallway. He washed up, brushed his teeth and straightened his tie. He gave his dark hair a few perfunctory passes with a brush and returned to the office.

His sports jacket was hanging on the back of a chair. As he shrugged into it, he flipped the calendar page to the next day's date, June 7. Scrawled on it was a note to himself: "Announce winner of contest and name of new line." Tomorrow? He'd completely forgotten about the contest. His mind assimilated the reminder, automatically inserting it into the evening's priorities. It gave him a reason to delay going home to his neat, silent house.

Bending, he took out a key and unlocked the bottom desk drawer. In a metal box at the back of the drawer was the winner's name and address and the name chosen for the new line of automobiles that National Motors would be manufacturing in its Neptune plant. The contest winner had suggested that they name the new line Neptune, after the town. The judges, three NM executives in the Detroit office, had been taken with the idea.

Joe reached for the telephone and dialed the newspaper office. "Is Ed still there? It's Joe Underwood at the NM plant."

Edgar Rankin, editor-reporter-photographer for the *American*, the local weekly, came on the line. "Hey, Joe, you just caught me. I was half out the door. What's up?"

"We're announcing the winner of our contest tomorrow. I'm going to his house this evening to give him the good news in person. Want to come along and get a picture?"

"You bet! Nice human interest for next Thursday's front page. Who's the lucky stiff?"

Joe consulted the piece of paper in his hand. "Some guy named Robert Roundtree. Keep it quiet until tomorrow, will you?"

"Old Bo?" Joe could tell by Ed's voice that he was grinning. "That old dude's become a professional contest entrant since he retired. He won a portable TV and a year's supply of mushroom soup last winter."

"Well, now he's won a chance to make a television commercial. I hope he's photogenic."

"Bo?" Ed laughed. "Yeah, I can see it. He's kind of a rustic philosopher type. Hey, that'll be something, Bo on TV. What time did you want to go over there?"

"About seven. I have to grab a bite to eat first. I can pick you up at your house at a quarter of."

"Fine. See ya." Ed was chuckling as he hung up.

Andrea Darnell braked at Neptune's only stoplight. There was a streak of yellow enamel on her left cheek, she noted as she aimed an idle glance at the van's side view mirror. She'd been in too big a hurry to leave the Wilburn house, her current job site, to clean up and change out of her paint-speckled coveralls. It was five-twenty, and she still had to stop for the mail and pick up Tony's birthday cake before going home.

Her fingers drummed on the steering wheel, keeping time with the country singer's lament coming from the van radio. *A woman's a fool to trust a man,* wailed the female vocalist. Andy tended to agree with her.

The light turned green, and Andy made a left turn and whipped into the post office parking lot. She'd arrived just in time, since the postal windows closed at five-thirty. *You told me I could count on you, but you lied,* moaned the nasal radio voice. "You said it, lady," Andy muttered as she flipped off the radio and climbed out.

The white and gold letters on the van's blue side read:

Quality Custom Painting and Paperhanging
Neptune, Nebraska
Interior and Exterior
Residential and Commercial
Free Estimates
Call us last for the best price.

Two years ago, after her divorce, Andy had taken over the business from her father, a move that coincided with Bo's decision to retire. She had returned to Neptune with her two sons and leased a house next door to her father's. She had never regretted the decision. Thanks to Bo's training, she did her job well and made enough to support her family comfortably if not lavishly. There were other pluses, too. She liked being her own boss, and her father was handy to keep an eye on the boys when he was needed. Now that summer vacation had started, she appreciated Bo's presence next door more than ever.

There was a line at the post office window. Scanning the backs and profiles of the three people ahead of her, she realized that she didn't know any of them.

Since the opening of the new automobile plant three months ago, hundreds of workers had arrived to swell the small town's population and give its retail businesses, including Andy's, a welcome infusion of new money.

Finally she reached the window. Bobby Cannon, the young clerk, grinned at her. "Hi, Andy. Forget your box key again?"

She gave him an apologetic smile. "Yeah, would you mind, Bobby?"

"That's what I'm here for." The clerk went over to the wall of boxes and pulled out a fistful of mail. "Looks like Bo's still entering contests," he remarked as he handed it to her.

"Keeps him off the streets," Andy murmured as she riffled through the envelopes.

Bobby laughed. "But not out of the domino parlor, right?"

"I don't know what Dad and his cronies would do without their domino games," Andy agreed.

"I hear they're gonna announce the winner of that car-naming contest tomorrow. Did Bo enter?"

National Motors, the U.S. automobile maker that had built a plant in Neptune, had been running a local contest for the past three months to name its new line. "He'd turned in thirty-one entries the last time I asked," Andy replied. "He claims there's a psychological advantage to the judges' seeing an entrant's name over and over."

"He must've read that in one of those contest magazines," Bobby said.

Andy nodded absently. "Thanks, Bobby." She finished looking through the mail as she returned to the van.

She got in and tossed the envelopes on the seat beside her. There was nothing for Tony from his father, not even a card.

"Terrific." Andy started the engine and burned rubber as she pulled out of the lot. "Damn it, Harley, can't you even remember your own son's birthday?" Obviously not, she answered herself silently. So what else was new? Andy could no longer recall what attractions she had once seen in her ex-husband, but she was sure that dependability hadn't been one of them.

She could picture Tony tearing open his presents later that evening, searching for something from his father. He'd realize there was nothing and look at her with that woeful, accusing expression in his blue eyes, as though she were somehow responsible.

What would she tell him this time? I'm sure there's a mistake. Maybe your father's gift was lost in the mail. Or, your father's a busy man, sweetheart. It must've slipped his mind. He'll think of it in a few days and feel awful.

She sighed, remembering that she'd used every one of those excuses before. It was getting more and more difficult to explain away Harley's lapses.

Andy found a parking place half a block from the bakery. As she passed the hardware store, a display of camping equipment caught her eye. She backtracked for a better look at the red, navy and green waterproof hiker's packs in one corner of the window. They appeared to be lightweight yet large enough for extra

clothing, camera gear and snacks. Numerous zippered outer pockets were covered by storm flaps to
keep out moisture. The shoulder straps and waist belt
were padded and adjustable. Tony would love one of
those.

She hesitated only another instant before going into
the hardware store. She bought the red pack and a
birthday card which she signed, "Dad," in sloppy,
looped handwriting that looked like Harley's. She had
the clerk gift wrap the present, but left off the bow,
reasoning that a package sent through the mail
wouldn't have one. Then she picked up the birthday
cake—chocolate with fudge icing and a yellow-and-
green candy cowboy with Happy Birthday, Tony!
spelled out inside his lasso.

It was six o'clock by the time she pulled into her
driveway. Tony burst from the house as she got out of
the van. "You're late!" he called as he ran down the
porch steps.

"Couldn't be helped. There was a line at the post
office." She thrust the gift-wrapped parcel at him.
"Here, carry this."

Tony's blue eyes were enormous circles in his
freckled face. "What is it?"

Andy reached back in the van for the cake box and
the mail, which was now strewn over the floor. "Your
guess is as good as mine. It came in the mail for you."

Tony was turning the package over and over.
"There's no name or address."

"I tore off the outer wrapping," Andy said, hoping that God would forgive her for lying to her child.

"I bet it's from Dad!" Tony squealed. "Can I open it now? Please!"

Andy grinned and climbed the porch steps with Tony hot on her heels. "No way. The presents don't get opened till we cut the cake, after dinner. You know the rules."

"Aw, Mom, I'll die if I have to wait that long," Tony groaned.

"We'll give you a nice funeral."

Tony groaned again, but gave up.

Andy dropped the mail on the couch and set the cake box beside it. "Where's Brad?"

"Helping Grandpa cook my birthday dinner. They wouldn't let me in the kitchen, but I could smell fried chicken."

Over Andy's objections, Bo had insisted on cooking Tony's birthday dinner at his house. Now Andy was glad he had. It had been a long day, and she felt tired and gritty. "You can take the present and your cake next door. I'm going to shower. Tell Pop I'll be there in half an hour."

"Hurry!" Tony pleaded.

"I'm hurrying." Andy laughed as she shut the bathroom door behind her. Then she opened the door again and thrust her head out. "No fair peeling back the Scotch tape for a peek at the box. And I will definitely notice if you make little slits in the wrapping paper with a razor blade like you did last Christmas."

Tony's chin dropped. "How'd you know?"

"Mothers know everything," Andy said mysteriously and shut the door.

She heard the front door slam as Tony left, then quiet descended on the house. She turned on the shower before stripping off her work clothes and tossing them in the hamper. She scrubbed the yellow enamel off her face with a cotton swab moistened with a special cleanser. Then she pulled the combs and pins from her thick auburn hair and shook it out as she stepped beneath the warm shower spray.

Closing her eyes, she tilted her head back and let the water pour over her face and through her hair. She stood like that for several moments before reaching for a bar of soap and lathering herself. Sore muscles slowly relaxed, and the tiredness seemed to seep out of her pores and drain away with the water.

Minutes later, she stepped out on the mat and, grabbing a thick blue towel, rubbed herself briskly. She styled her shoulder-length hair with a brush and hair drier and caught it back at the temples with two combs. There wasn't time for makeup, so she merely made two passes at her lips with pink gloss before dressing in the first thing that her hands pulled from the closet—jeans and a faded red shirt that Harley had discarded long before their separation. The boys and Bo probably wouldn't notice what she wore, anyway.

It was six-thirty by the time she grabbed her keys and Bo's mail and went next door. By six forty-five, Tony had polished off a drumstick, mashed potatoes and gravy and English peas and was urging his brother, mother and grandfather to finish eating so he could cut the cake.

"Give us a break," Brad groaned, reaching for a second piece of crisp fried chicken. He was a sturdy twelve-year-old with a growing boy's insatiable appetite. Like Tony, Brad was freckled and sandy-haired, but his eyes were brown with hazel flecks, resembling his father's.

"Mom, he's eating slow on purpose!" Tony accused.

"Tony," Andy said resignedly.

"He is! Tell him to hurry."

Andy exchanged an amused look with her father. "Has he been like this all day?"

"Only since noon," Bo said. He took a bite of potatoes and gravy and finished looking through the mail beside his plate. "Well, there's nothing here about the National Motors contest. I guess I didn't win."

"They aren't announcing the winner till tomorrow, Grandpa," Brad said.

"But you'd think they'd let the winner know ahead of time," Bo said glumly.

"They didn't let you know at all when you won the fifteenth prize in that magazine sweepstakes," Brad reminded him. "The toaster oven just came in the mail, and you had to look through your records to find out which contest you'd won. Remember?"

"That's right." Bo seemed encouraged by Brad's words.

Tony plopped his elbows on the table, rested his chin in one hand and glared at his grandfather as Bo ladled more peas on his plate. Andy put down her fork. "Come out to the kitchen with me, birthday boy, and help me light the candles."

Tony yelped gleefully and clambered out of his chair. Finally, the candles were blown out and the cake cut, and Tony pounced on his presents and began ripping off paper. He was delighted with the Swiss army knife from Brad, the board game from Bo, and the new bike seat and reflector from Andy. But the hit of the evening was the hiker's pack. Tony zipped and unzipped every compartment a dozen times, oohing and aahing. "Look, Mom, there's a place just the right size for my thermos bottle.... My first aid kit will go here.... Grandpa, isn't it great? I knew Dad wouldn't forget my birthday."

Andy gathered up the discarded wrapping paper and took it to the kitchen trash can. Bo followed, carrying dirty dishes in both hands. "You wash, and I'll dry," he told Andy.

"The meal was delicious, Pop." Andy plunged both hands into the soapy water on one side of the double sink. She washed a bowl and deposited it in the rinse water on the other side of the sink. Bo fished out the bowl and dried it slowly. "All in all," Andy mused, "I think Tony's birthday was a success."

"He sure likes that backpack," Bo observed.

"Hmmm," Andy agreed.

"Looks an awful lot like one I saw in the window of the hardware store yesterday."

Andy darted a startled look at him. "Tony wasn't with you, was he?"

"No."

Andy breathed a sigh of relief. "Good."

After a long moment, Bo said, "I know why you bought it, Andy, but how long are you going to keep covering up for Harley? I'll bet they don't even know their father hasn't sent a support check for six months."

"Oh, Dad, we can get along without the child support if we have to. I just couldn't stand for Tony to be disappointed on his birthday. I heard him last week bragging to one of his friends about Harley, saying that his father always sends him the neatest birthday presents."

"Ah, honey, I know you'd like to protect those boys from ever being hurt, but you can't do it." He put down the dish towel and patted her shoulder.

Andy turned, wrapped her arms around his ample middle and rested her head on his shoulder. "I'm glad they have you, Pop. I'm glad I have you." She squeezed him fiercely, then stepped back. "Now, let's finish these dishes before I start bawling."

"Grandpa." Brad came into the kitchen. "There're two men here to see you. One of them's Mr. Rankin from the newspaper. It's important, they said."

Andy followed her father into the living room. Skinny, stoop-shouldered Edgar Rankin reminded Andy of a stork. Although his father was still listed on the *American*'s masthead as managing editor and publisher, in actuality Edgar did most of the work. Old man Rankin spent more time at the domino parlor with Bo and a half dozen other retired men than he did at the newspaper office. Edgar had a camera in his hand and was grinning from ear to ear.

With Edgar was a tall, dark-haired man of about thirty-five. "Are you Mr. Roundtree?" he asked, his gray eyes assessing Bo.

The two men shook hands. "That's me."

"I'm Joe Underwood, director of marketing over at the NM plant. It's my pleasure to tell you that you won our contest. We'll be using the name you entered on our new line."

"Yaaa!" Tony jumped up and down.

"Hey, Grandpa, didn't I tell you not to give up?"

Bo beamed. "You did, Brad. Which name did you choose? I sent in thirty-three."

Joe was quickly taking mental stock of Round-tree's physical characteristics. Thick, iron-gray hair, a round, squashed-looking nose, shaggy brown eyebrows that hadn't grayed at all, and lively blue eyes. He wore striped overalls with a green checked shirt. Roundtree's voice was a slow country drawl. With the right lines and delivery, he could be perfect, Joe thought. If they could just capture that unsophisticated, down-home essence on film.

"The judges chose Neptune," Joe said.

"I kinda liked that one myself," Bo agreed.

"Is Grandpa going to be on television?" Tony asked.

Joe smiled at the freckle-faced boy. This one's full of mischief, Joe thought. Must be nine or ten, the rambunctious age. David would've been ten if—Joe chopped off the thought viciously. "Looks like it," he said. "We won't know for sure until we make the screen test."

"These are my grandsons," Bo said. "Tony and Brad. And my daughter, Andy."

The woman had been standing behind her father until then. She stepped into view, and Joe gave her a quick, sweeping glance. Her face was classically oval, her skin honey-toned with a faint sprinkling of gold-en freckles across her small nose. Her mouth was beautifully shaped, sensuous without being too full. Her hair was thick and richly auburn, falling loosely over her shoulders in carelessly sweeping waves. Her brows were dark and arched, and beneath them her eyes, shaded by thick lashes, were an electric blue. She wore no makeup, but with that face she didn't need any.

"Hello, Mr. Underwood."

Her voice was full throated, with just a hint of the slow drawl that was so pronounced in her father's words. Joe found it sexy, and suddenly he wanted a cigarette. "Joe," he said and let his eyes sweep down. She was tall, about five nine, he estimated. Tight jeans revealed long, slender legs. The man's shirt she wore hid the shape of her upper body, making Joe feel cheated. He wondered if the rest of her body could possibly live up to those legs.

"What're you doing here, Ed?" Bo asked the newspaper man.

"Hey, I came to get your picture for the paper." Edgar Rankin had a habit of punctuating his dialogue with "hey."

"Well, shoot, give me a chance to put on my suit."

Ed held his camera to his eye, adjusting the focus. "Hey, you look fine like that."

"Nobody would recognize you in your suit, Pop," Andy put in.

"Brad, turn on those table lamps," Ed said. "Stand over there away from the door, Bo."

As Ed snapped several shots of Bo, Joe conversed with the boys. Andy sat on the padded arm of a chair and watched. Bo kept protesting that he'd break Ed's camera, but she could tell he enjoyed being the center of attention.

Her glance slid to Joe Underwood, who was lounging against the back of the couch. He gave the impression of being at ease, but at the same time sharply alert. Brad was telling him about his baseball team, and Tony kept interrupting to show Joe his birthday presents. Joe talked easily with the boys. He's good with kids, Andy thought, and wondered if he had children of his own.

Leisurely she studied him. The expensive tan sports jacket hung open, and his tie was askew. His hands were tucked casually into the pockets of brown trousers. He doesn't spend much time thinking about clothes, she reflected. The prominent bone structure of his face was quintessentially male without being classically handsome. The gray eyes that had studied her when she and Joe were introduced were intelligent and very watchful. For an instant, she wished that she'd worn something a little more flattering than Harley's old shirt.

"That about does it, Bo," Ed was saying as he fitted a cover over the camera lens. "I'll print you up a set of these, if you'd like."

"Aw, I don't think so—"

"Thanks, Ed," Andy interrupted. "I'd like to have a set."

Bo looked faintly embarrassed but pleased.

"Mom, can Joe and Mr. Rankin have a piece of my birthday cake?" Tony asked.

Andy could feel Joe Underwood's eyes on her as she turned away from Ed and her father. "Sure." She met his look briefly, then slid off the chair arm and went into the kitchen, wishing that Tony hadn't made the offer. For some reason, Joe Underwood's attention made her feel uncomfortable.

Andy brought the cake and coffee in on a tray and served the visitors. In her absence, all the seating space in the living room had been occupied, leaving only one armchair vacant. Joe Underwood sat in the other armchair, which was angled toward the empty one with a narrow space between. Bo was telling Ed a long-winded tale about a humorous incident from his youth, which had gotten wilder in his memory as he had gotten older. Andy had heard the story many times before, and so had Brad and Tony, but the boys hung on their grandfather's words as though this were the first time.

"Your father's a natural storyteller," Joe said as he cut a bite of cake.

Holding a cup of coffee, Andy eased into the armchair. "He's a ham."

Joe's eyes, over the rim of his cup, were amused. "That's good. Maybe he won't freeze in front of a camera."

Andy chuckled. "I don't think you need worry about that."

He liked her deep, throaty laugh. He ate more cake, then set the plate down on the floor beside his chair. "I promised your boys they could watch the screen test. I hope that's all right. I'm not sure yet when it'll be. We have to bring a crew down from New York."

She shrugged and sipped her coffee. "Fine."

"You're invited, too."

"Thanks, but I'll probably be working." She watched him set down his cup, take out a cigarette and look around for an ashtray. "We don't have any," Andy said. "You can use your saucer."

"Sure you don't mind?"

"Not at all."

He lit up, took a long drag, and said casually, "Those are two nice kids."

"Thank you. I happen to agree."

He eyed her through a plume of smoke. "Do you have a husband, Andy?"

The question took her off guard. She met his watchful gaze with a frown. "Why?"

He noted her sudden defensive stiffening. "Idle curiosity."

There was nothing idle in the way his eyes held hers. "I'm divorced," she said finally.

"You live here with your father?"

More idle curiosity? she wondered. "No." She felt oddly reluctant to go beyond the simple answer to his question. There was something about him, something that made her too painfully aware of her unflattering attire and lack of makeup. The way he looked at her made her sure that he missed very little. She was conscious of a wariness within her, as though he posed some kind of threat.

When he spoke again, the words were so low that she was certain for an instant that she couldn't have heard correctly. "Do you have a lover?"

In the next instant, she knew that she hadn't been mistaken. She managed not to choke on her coffee. "Dozens," she shot back and smiled sweetly in case anybody else was looking. "Is this another one of your contests? Then let's compare notes. How many do you have?"

So she could hold her own, Joe thought. She might appear fragile in that shirt that swallowed her, but she wasn't. Though he was annoyed by her refusal to tell him more about herself, he admitted that he deserved the sharp retort.

He acknowledged her thrust with a grin. "Point taken. I was out of line."

"That's true," she murmured with the ghost of a smile. "I'm glad we understand each other."

He took another drag on his cigarette. "Do we?" The question was delivered in an odd tone that seemed somehow to challenge her. "I'm thinking of things I don't understand about you, but would like to."

Andy emptied her cup and cradled it in her lap. She wadded her napkin and placed it in the cup. "That sounds like an invitation."

"If it is?"

"I'd have to say no." Restlessly, she crossed one ankle over the other. Her eyes were cloudy.

"Aren't you even curious about what sort of invitation I might be issuing?"

"No. It's not all that hard to figure out." She plucked at the collar of her faded, oversize shirt. "I may look like I just fell off a cabbage truck, but in this case looks are deceiving."

He laughed. From across the room, the newspaperman raised his voice. "Hey, Joe, you ready to go?"

Bending forward, Joe ground out his cigarette in the saucer, which he set on a lamp table. He rose, letting his gaze skim over Andy before he met her eyes. "You look more like a woman who just stepped out of a bath or a bed." He smiled at the soft color that suffused her cheeks, surprised at how reluctant he was to leave. When was the last time he'd seen a woman blush? But it wasn't merely the woman, though she intrigued him. It was the atmosphere of family in the house that he'd sensed from the moment he arrived. "I'm sure we'll see each other again."

"I don't see how we can avoid it," Andy replied. "This is a small town." She waited until he had crossed the room, said goodbye to Bo and the boys, and followed Ed Rankin from the house before she stirred from her chair.

Interesting man, she mused. Smart-mouthed but interesting. Well, she had once thought that Harley was interesting, and she'd ended up being incredibly bored. Somehow she didn't think a woman would ever be bored by Joe Underwood.

There was an aura of sadness, almost of tragedy about him. She was startled by the thought and shook it off quickly. She wasn't interested in Joe. There was no room for a man in her life, and certainly not for a man with problems.

Chapter Two

Groggily, Joe crawled out of bed. A dull headache throbbed at the back of his eyes. He knew from the position of the sun outside his bedroom window that he'd overslept. The red numerals pulsing on his clock-radio dial said 8:20. He hadn't set the alarm because he hadn't overslept since moving to Neptune. He was always in his office by seven-thirty, sometimes earlier. Until today.

He staggered into the bathroom and downed two aspirin tablets with water straight from the faucet. Then he turned the shower on cold and, clenching his teeth, stepped in.

"Agghhh!"

Every muscle in his body locked rigidly. He forced himself to stand there for a full minute while he counted slowly. Cold water is character building, Underwood, he told himself. When he'd counted to sixty, he turned the temperature control to warm. His muscles slowly relaxed. He was fully awake now, and the warm water felt wonderful. He reached for the soap.

So he'd overslept. He was entitled. He put in more overtime than anybody else at the plant on the management level. Besides, he'd had a bad night. For the first couple of hours, he'd lain awake, strangely exhilarated by that brief exchange with Andy Darnell.

He knew what his problem was—he hadn't had a woman in two years, and hadn't wanted one. Well, only lately and not often. But whenever his physical urges had threatened to demolish his self-control, he'd buried them in work. So, last night he was ripe for Andy Darnell's oddball brand of charm. Even in that disreputable masculine shirt, she was the sexiest thing he'd seen in a long time.

But she wasn't interested. She'd made that clear. Damn it, he had no right to be, either. The thought depressed him. He knew that it came from unreasoning guilt, but knowing the feeling was illogical didn't keep it from crouching at the back of his mind, ready to pounce whenever he noticed an attractive woman.

The company psychologist, whom he'd visited a few times in Detroit, had reminded him that his feelings had nothing to do with true guilt. They were a punishment that he inflicted on himself for the crime of being alive, and sexual attraction was an essential part of human existence. He must put the past behind him, the counselor had said, and start a new life.

As was the case with most sensible advice, it was easier said than done. Work had proved the best antidote, but sometimes the feelings that he managed to push down during the day erupted in nightmares like the one he'd had last night. He'd finally gone to sleep after midnight, but he'd awakened at three, moaning and thrashing. He'd lain in the dark, his body bathed in sweat and his heart pounding, and relived the dream.

He was standing in an observation area at the Detroit airport when a jet touched down on the runway and rolled toward the terminal. As he watched, the jet burst into flames. He ran toward the flight gate and into the tunnel, but four men grabbed him from behind and dragged him back. He tried to fight free, but they were too many for him. They took him back to the observation area. When he looked at the burning plane again, he saw two small faces at the window. The faces were convulsed with weeping as they pleaded for rescue and they were looking straight at him. When the men who were holding him let him go, he leaped for the huge plate glass wall that overlooked the runway. He hit the glass and heard it shatter and then he jerked awake.

Once he'd oriented himself, he had left the bed, which was damp with his perspiration, and smoked a cigarette, but it was after five before he could sleep again.

The nightmares had a horrible sameness—the plane was on the runway when it burst into flames—even though it hadn't happened that way at all. Their plane had crashed in the Rocky Mountains in a turbulent rainstorm. It had exploded, but it hadn't burned. It wouldn't have mattered if it had, because everybody

on board had been killed on impact. If he'd been with
them, he couldn't have saved them or himself. It was
senseless to feel guilty because he'd been spared.

These were the same arguments he always used on
himself, and as usual it took about fifteen minutes
before he could convince himself, at the gut level, of
their truth and put such thoughts out of his mind. By
that time he'd shaved and dressed in a lightweight navy
suit, white shirt and red-and-navy striped tie. He
didn't take time to make coffee, since his secretary
would have made a pot at the office. He grabbed an
apple from the bowl on the kitchen table just before he
went out the back door.

He got into his black sedan and backed out. As he
reached the street, he noticed a painter in white coveralls standing on a tall extension ladder next to a
house a few doors down. The painter wore a white cap
from which a thick cascade of hair was escaping. From
his car the hair appeared to be a rich auburn. Joe
dropped the apple on the seat beside him, took his foot
off the brake and eased forward.

Andy climbed down off the ladder to refill her
plastic bucket with yellow paint from a gallon can.
Before she opened the can, she stepped back to ad-
mire her handiwork. She'd be finished with this side
by noon, and then she'd have only the back and the
shutters to do. The soft yellow paint—"pure cream"
it was called—combined with white shutters was going
to make the Wilburn house look a hundred percent
better than the old dull green exterior.

When she'd brought the paint sample cards to the
house, Joyce Wilburn had chosen something called

"canary yellow." Andy had had the devil's own time making Joyce believe that a whole house covered with canary would be so bright a person would have to wear sunglasses to look at it. She'd had to cover a third of the south side of the house with canary before Joyce was convinced. That was all right, though, because it was taking two coats to cover the old green, anyway. Yes, Andy told herself, pure cream was exactly right for the Wilburns's two-story Victorian.

She sighed, picked up a screwdriver and pried the lid off the paint can. She half filled the plastic bucket, then decided to have a cup of iced tea from her thermos before starting again. She poured the tea and leaned back against the ladder so that she was half sitting on a conveniently placed rung. She crossed her ankles, closed her eyes and took a swallow of the cold, sweet tea.

"I don't believe it."

The deep male voice made her jump so hard tea splashed out of her cup and soaked the bib of her coveralls. Her eyes flew open. Joe Underwood was standing in front of her, his hands thrust deeply into the pockets of navy trousers, his open suit coat pushed back by his arms. His neatly brushed dark hair was still damp from the shower. His face was smooth and still ruddy from his morning shave, and he smelled of spicy cologne. He looked even better to Andy than he'd looked last night. If there was one thing she didn't need, though, it was a man, this man in particular, looking so darned good and smiling at her like that, his eyes all crinkled at the corners. She was painfully aware of her loose coveralls and untidy hair and perspiring face. Her nose was probably shining like one of Tony's new bicycle reflectors!

"You nearly scared the wits out of me!"

"Sorry." He didn't look sorry. He looked amused, maybe even delighted with having slipped up on her.

She took another drink of tea and tried to poke her hair back under her cap with her free hand. "What don't you believe?"

"You're a house painter."

"Obviously."

He watched her drain her cup and screw it back on the thermos that stood beside the ladder. There was a suggestion of a slender waist and tight rear as she bent to set the thermos down, but when she straightened, even that suggestion was gone. The coveralls fit loosely—eminently practical for a painter. But, damn it, he wished he could see her in something besides sloppy shirts and coveralls. Curiosity about the body hidden beneath her clothes tantalized him like the smell of food tantalizes a starving man. "You're also a paperhanger. I read the advertising on your van last night. You live next door to Bo."

The last was said almost accusingly, as though she'd lied to him about where her home was. "You're just full of brilliant deductions this morning. Tell me, did you ever think of becoming a private eye?"

He acknowledged the sarcasm with a shrug. Tiny beads of perspiration lined the skin above her upper lip. Why did he find that sensual? "Nope. I like what I do."

She lifted a brow. "So do I."

"How did you get into this line of work?"

"It was my father's business. He trained me before he retired."

"Are you going to train your sons to take over from you?"

She folded her arms in front of her and leaned back against the ladder. "It's okay with me if that's what they want to do—after they graduate from college." She straightened, picked up the plastic bucket and rested one canvas-shod, crepe-soled foot on the bottom rung of the ladder. "Do you live around here?"

He gestured without looking away from her. "The white house with the screened porch at the end of the block."

"Oh."

From out of nowhere came a strong impulse to touch her, but he managed to keep his hands in his pockets. "You have paint on the end of your nose."

She looked into his eyes, her expression grave, as though she had somehow guessed his thoughts. "I'll have it all over me before the day is through." Her gaze slid away from his. "Aren't you late for work?"

He nearly laughed. He wondered if he made her feel as restless as she made him feel. He shifted his feet. "Trying to get rid of me?"

"I'm busy." She stood waiting, one foot still on the ladder.

"When will you be not busy?"

She considered this while lifting the bucket, which was getting heavy, to rest it on a rung. "I quit work at five o'clock. Then I have to go to the post office. Then I'll go home and cook dinner. After that I promised I'd take Brad and Tony to a movie."

He understood that she was telling him she had no time for him. He'd never experienced a brush-off before and he didn't like it. "What about tomorrow night? Saturday."

"I know what tomorrow is." She steadied the paint bucket. "Are you asking me for a date?"

"You know damned well that's what I'm doing."

All at once, she felt faintly light-headed. She took a deep breath. "I have to ask you something. I hope you don't mind."

"Go ahead."

"Do you have a wife or a girlfriend back where you came from?" She couldn't imagine that there wasn't a woman somewhere for a man like Joe Underwood, maybe several women.

So that's what she thought of him, what she'd been thinking all along. He tried to speak casually, but it came out between his clenched teeth. "If I did, I wouldn't be asking you to go out with me."

She looked at him steadily for a long moment before she said, "I'm sorry if I insulted you."

"Apology accepted. Now, about Saturday night..."

"I don't date."

"What do you mean you don't date?"

"Exactly that. It doesn't require an explanation."

He shook his head. "You don't date. You mean like never?"

"I haven't had a date since before I was married."

Neither had he. He might have said the words, but it would probably cause her to ask more questions. Was he divorced? Widowed? This wasn't the time or the place to go into that. "Then isn't it about time you had some?'' There was a wicked twinkle in his gray eyes. ''Dates, I mean.''

She tucked her bottom lip between her teeth for an instant. ''I don't get it. Why me?''

His quick grin was mischievous. ''Because I want to find out if you own a dress.'' Her smile encouraged him. ''Look, I'm asking you to have dinner with me. That's all.''

Her smile deepened. Last night she'd told herself she wanted nothing to do with Joe Underwood. But at the moment she couldn't think of any good reason why she shouldn't go to dinner with him. It wasn't a lifetime commitment, for heaven's sake. ''Well, then, I guess I'd better borrow a dress.''

He pulled a hand from his pocket, reached out and tucked a damp tendril of auburn hair behind her ear, then let his fingertips rest on the curve of her cheek. He'd done it before he was even aware that he was going to. He just wanted to touch her before he left. She was surprised, he could tell, but she didn't pull away. She merely gazed at him with a confused look in her blue eyes. Or perhaps he only imagined the confusion. He dropped his hand. ''I'll pick you up at seven.'' Without waiting for a reply, he turned and walked quickly toward the car parked at the curb. He was whistling as he got in and drove away.

Andy stared after him, a little dazed. Heat shimmered in the air, making the street and the black sedan look out of focus, as though in a dream. She started up the ladder, and reality returned with a harsh jolt.

Dear heaven, she'd agreed to go out with him. *Now* she thought of several reasons why she should have said no. Joe Underwood was clearly what the media called upwardly mobile. Neptune was only a stop on his way to the top, probably a brief stop at that.

She had no business getting involved with somebody who would be moving on. Not that one date was getting involved; it was just that it was pointless. Then there was that hint of tragedy she'd seen last night, which could mean almost anything—he was madly in love with somebody who didn't love him, he was a compulsive gambler or an alcoholic, he was embezzling company funds ... anything.

She dipped her brush and applied paint with smooth, even strokes. Okay, she didn't really believe Joe Underwood was doing any of those terrible things, but she still shouldn't be going out with him.

Why was she?

A wry smile tugged at the corners of her mouth as she dipped the brush again. The plain fact was that she'd enjoyed talking to him last night and again today. He was quick, clever, amusing. Most of her conversations were with preteen boys or elderly men. The prospect of a whole evening of conversation with a man her own age had been too tempting to turn down.

As long as she was going, she told herself, she might as well enjoy it.

Andy didn't borrow a dress for Saturday night, but after looking through her closet and realizing that she hadn't had a new dress since her divorce, she bought one. Neptune's shops didn't offer a wide variety, but she finally settled on a pale blue cotton with a full skirt, fitted waist and wide bands of white lace edging the deeply scooped neck and narrow cap sleeves. It was, she decided, softly feminine without being too dressy. With it she'd wear her white sandals and no jewelry except for a small puffed heart on a silver neck chain.

Bo was delighted that she was going out with Joe and offered to keep the boys at his house overnight. "That way," he told her, "you won't have to worry about getting in early."

Andy hid a smile. "I don't plan to stay out late in any case, Pop, but the boys can stay overnight."

Saturday evening she sent Tony and Brad next door at six, giving herself time for a long bubble bath. Joe arrived at seven, wearing a straw-colored sports jacket with an open-collared chocolate brown shirt and trousers.

As he stepped on the porch, she came out of the house and smiled at him. "Hi." She turned back to lock the door, giving him a chance to study her. To say he wasn't disappointed would have been vastly understating the case.

Unobserved, he let his eyes wander up her body, taking in the smooth line of narrow feet and ankles and just a hint of lean, firm calves beneath the full hem of her dress, a waist so slender a man could span it easily with two hands, and a sideways glimpse small, firm breasts thrusting against blue fabric.

As she bent to fit her key in the lock, her thick auburn hair swung, brushing her shoulders. She wore it loose, parted in the middle and swept back to fall in careless waves. He studied her profile. The nose was small and straight, the mouth pink, moist, the lips slightly parted as they might be in passion. Something coiled slowly in his stomach. Desire.

She turned and dropped her key into a small white clutch. Discovering that his throat was dry, Joe swallowed quickly. "Ready?"

She came toward him, and he cupped her elbow as they went down the steps. It seemed natural then to let his hand slide down and link with hers. She looked over at him quickly, but left her hand in his. "Where are we going?"

"Banner's. I've eaten everywhere in town, and they have the best dinners."

Banner's was a rustic steak house about a mile south of town. The restaurant was said to have a romantic atmosphere, which meant that they had such dim lighting it was possible to stumble into a table before you realized it was there. But Banner's did serve good mesquite grilled steaks, and Andy was famished, having had nothing since the peanut butter sandwich she'd eaten at noon.

Joe handed her into the car, and she sank into the softness and rich smell of leather. "Is your father sitting with Brad and Tony?" Joe asked as they drove away from the house.

"Yes. They're—" She had been about to say that they were spending the night with Bo, but something in Joe's expression stopped her. She might not have been seeing any men since her divorce, but she could still recognize sexual tension. It wasn't all on Joe's side, either. When she'd stepped out on the porch to greet him, and he'd smiled at her in that slow, lazy way, her heart had done a little flip-flop. She'd liked the feel of his long fingers entwined with hers, too. Perhaps it would be better, when he took her home later, if he didn't know her house was empty.

"They're what?" Joe asked.

"Uh, they're going to make popcorn and play Monopoly. Pop gave the game to Tony for his birthday."

"Yeah, he showed me his birthday presents the other night. He sure was proud of that backpack his Dad sent him. Do they get to see their father often?"

"No. Harley lives in Florida. At least he did the last time we heard from him. That was six months ago." Andy halted abruptly, wishing she could call back the words. Joe glanced over at her questioningly. She put her head back against the car seat and sighed. "I don't know why I'm running on about this to you."

"Wasn't there a note with Tony's birthday gift? At least a return address?"

"No." She hesitated. "Actually, there wasn't even a gift. I bought the backpack and told Tony it was from Harley. I didn't want him to be disappointed." She glanced at Joe, but he was looking straight ahead. He said nothing. "I sense disapproval. You don't think I should have done it, do you?"

"It's none of my business."

"Right," she murmured. When he didn't respond, she went on, "If you had kids, you'd understand why—you don't have any kids, do you?"

"No."

The word was clipped out, as sharp as a razor, and the atmosphere in the car suddenly felt cold. "I'm sorry,'' Andy faltered. "I—did I say something wrong?''

She could actually feel that he was forcing himself to relax. "No."

"It's just that I assumed you must've been married at some point."

He drew in a deep breath and let it out. "I was."

"Oh. Then you're divorced."

She sensed him stiffen again. "She died. Almost two years ago." The words were toneless and seemed to hang between them like stones on a string. They explained the sadness she'd felt in him, and it was evident that he didn't want to talk about his wife. Andy's thoughts scurried about for another subject, but her mind was a total blank. To think that she'd looked forward to their conversation this evening! Fortunately they reached Banner's then, and she didn't have to find something to say immediately.

They ordered steaks, and Joe asked the waiter to bring them a bottle of the best red wine. "You look lovely tonight," he said as he filled her wineglass.

"Thank you. And I even own this dress." They smiled at each other and lifted their glasses, and after that everything was easier, more relaxed. Maybe it was the dim lighting, or the wine, but whatever it was, those tense moments in the car might never have happened.

Over perfectly grilled steaks, she learned that Joe had been raised in Montana, had attended a small college with a strong business program in a Washington suburb and upon graduation, had taken a job with National Motors in Detroit.

"Did you stay in Detroit until you moved to Neptune?"

He nodded. "I'd gone about as high as I could go without a hitch 'in the field,' as they call it. This job couldn't have come up at a better time, and I grabbed it."

She suspected that Detroit held too many memories of his wife and said quickly, "So, you don't plan to end your days in Neptune."

He chuckled. "I don't plan to, no. The usual scenario is for them to leave you in the field a year or two, and then, if you've proven you can handle it, they bring you back to Detroit in a management position."

Her grin was quick. "Trailing clouds of glory?"

He laughed. "Something like that. But I'm perfectly content in Neptune for now. It's much more casual and relaxed than the home office. You don't have to deal with all the political maneuvering, people consolidating their power bases and looking for ways to draw the CEO's attention. The relationship between the managers in the field is simple and straightforward. If somebody stabs you in the back it's because he thinks you've earned it, not because he's afraid you're after his job."

"Simple and straightforward. I see what you mean."

He watched her swirl the wine in her glass, then sip slowly. The shadowy lighting blurred the auburn curls falling over her shoulders and darkened the blue of her eyes. It accentuated the softness of her mouth and the dark shadow between her breasts where the silver heart lay.

Joe suffered from the same impulse to touch her that he'd noticed before. He was bewildered by it. He'd learned to suppress his impulses, yet he reached out and curled his fingers around the slender, ringless hand that rested, palm down, beside her plate.

She gazed at their hands for a moment and slowly lifted her eyes to his face. She gave him a small half smile. It wasn't flirtatious or coy. It was a simple acknowledgment of the attraction between them.

His thumb rubbed the back of her hand gently while he continued to gaze at her. Her hair looked so soft. He wanted to caress it, to feel it slip through his fingers. Tonight she'd applied makeup, but with a light hand and mostly around her eyes. Mascara accentuated the length and thickness of lashes that were already naturally lavish, and the effect was breathtaking.

Andy was too aware of the light, firm pressure of his hand and the seductive stroking of his thumb. Flushing, she pulled her gaze from his, then realized she'd been staring at his mouth. She glanced away, noticed her half-full glass and pulled her hand from his to reach for the wine. She gripped the stem too hard because her fingers seemed to be trembling.

"Would you like dessert?" he asked in a low tone that made her gaze dart back to his face. He was watching her intently.

She gave him an easy smile, but her pulse was pounding. "No."

"Neither do I." He tossed a bill on the table, more than enough to cover the meal. "Shall we go?"

She nodded, not trusting herself to speak just then because her throat felt too tight. She didn't utter a word until they were in the car. "Dinner was nice. Thank you."

"Would you like to go to a movie? Or we could stop by my place for a drink."

"No. I think I'd better go home now."

She's afraid of what will happen if she doesn't, Joe mused. Well, maybe it was best to pull in the reins. The sexual tension flowing between them was as thick as mulligan stew. He smoked a cigarette as he drove to her house. He walked her to the door, but when the final moment came, he couldn't let it go at that. There were lights on in Bo Roundtree's house, but Andy's windows were dark. Evidently the boys were next door.

"Will you ask me in?"

She looked up at him, her lovely features blurred by the night. "I don't think so, Joe. It—it could get too—too complicated. I don't want any complications."

"Maybe it wouldn't be as complicated as you think. We might find the fantasy is better than the reality."

She understood his meaning, but she didn't think he believed it any more than she did. She wasn't willing to test the theory, either. He touched her hair and slowly combed his fingers through it. Then he curved his hand lightly at the back of her neck. She looked up again, wary.

He could feel her pulse beating beneath his thumb. "We've both been thinking about this moment all evening," he said.

She didn't deny it. What was the point?

"A kiss is nice, but it's just a kiss. Since we've spent so much time wondering how it would be, we might as well find out, and then we can forget it."

She should have stopped it right there, but curiosity overcame her good sense. She *had* been wondering all evening how his firmly sculpted mouth would feel, how it would taste. If she didn't satisfy her curiosity, she would be up half the night wondering. She stared at his mouth in the darkness and saw a faint gleam of white. He was teasing her, or daring her. She didn't like one any better than the other. The flicker of annoyance that ran through her made up her mind. "You're right. A kiss is just a kiss." How earthshaking could a touching of lips be? Everybody did it. Kids not even out of braces did it.

He bent his head slowly, and just as slowly, she lifted her chin. Their lips met tentatively, lightly. She was surprised at how soft his were. It had been such a long time since a man had kissed her that she'd forgotten.

She was aware of curiosity and surprise. She was aware of the nice, masculine smell of his cologne, and the faint taste of tobacco and the wine they'd drunk. At some point amid all the discoveries, the kiss changed. She realized that her lips were parted to accept more, but she didn't remember when it had happened.

Her fingers clutched convulsively at his shirt collar, and she pressed closer to him, feeling the hardness of his chest against her breasts. His mouth heated on hers, and his hands came up to cup her head and tilt it so that he could take the kiss still deeper. That was the moment when she realized she'd made a mistake. A kiss wasn't just a kiss. But it was too late to do anything about it. She'd lost control of the situation. Worse, she reveled in her loss of control.

To Joe, she tasted warm and sweet. She fit his embrace perfectly, and her breasts pressing against his chest were driving him wild. How had he known it would be like this? Desire burned in him, and he was on the edge of losing what tenuous control he still clung to.

Joe lifted his head and set her away from him gently. His heart was thundering in his ears, and his mind was clouded with wanting her, but he had enough control to step back and mutter, "Now we know." His voice was none too steady, but she didn't seem to notice. "Good night."

Andy whispered, "Good night, Joe," and leaned her head back against the door to make her brain stop reeling.

He looked at her for another long moment, then turned and walked down the steps and into the blackness of the yard. Andy closed shaking fingers over her key and unlocked the door. Inside, in the darkness, she sagged against the wall. She felt weak, drained.

Now we know.

Though it was warm in the house, she shivered in the darkness. Just a simple good-night kiss, she thought. Your problem is you're not used to drinking, and three glasses of wine have made you giddy.

She couldn't quite convince herself.

Chapter Three

Andy went directly to bed, but not to sleep. After fifteen minutes of restless tossing, she got up, poured a glass of milk and found an old Bogart movie on television. This one hadn't been "updated" with the new colorizing technique that, in Andy's opinion, had ruined *The Maltese Falcon*.

She liked the intricate textures and delicate shadings of black and white in the old movies. There was more subtlety, more mystery, more left to the imagination, more faith in the viewer's ability to fill in the blanks. Black and white films allowed one to sit back and enjoy while remaining at whatever emotional distance one found comfortable. After all, it was easy to remind yourself at any point that what was on the screen wasn't real, full-color life, but only flickering shadows and images on film.

Technicolor could be too harsh, too mercilessly real. Too much reality could wear you out with its demands on your moods and emotions.

Like that kiss on the porch.

Now we know.

She should have known beforehand. She'd felt from the beginning that Joe Underwood was a complicated man. Hadn't she been intrigued by the layers she'd sensed in him the first time they'd talked? Hadn't she felt that peculiar, almost forgotten, ache when he touched her?

She couldn't remember ever being so affected by Harley's kisses. She hadn't known how to handle the wild sensations that had raced through her as Joe's mouth had heated on hers.

She was an ordinary woman with simple wants. Early in their relationship, she'd found Harley's lovemaking warm and pleasurable—comfortable. It was a natural activity to be enjoyed when the need arose, like eating or sleeping. Having had no previous experience, she'd assumed that that was what lovemaking was supposed to be.

Eventually, of course, the problems in her marriage had spoiled the lovemaking, as well as everything else. When she'd finally had it with being dragged all over the country, at the mercy of Harley's frequent job changes and impractical money-making schemes, she had made up her mind to leave him. She hadn't felt sexually deprived—she'd been too relieved at finally having a settled life. She was fed up with impossible dreams and longed for simplicity and structure.

There were things in life that were more important than a slow, burning kiss on a summer night. Particularly when she'd had too much wine to think straight. Particularly when she knew so little about the man. Particularly when he was still grieving for his dead wife.

The kiss had been a mistake, but it wasn't an irreparable one. She would mark it down to experience and forget it and what it had made her feel.

In the still night, Andy sat in her dark living room, with her knees drawn up under her gown, and focused her attention on the flickering images on the television screen. Bogart and Bacall bantering, romancing, loving. Before long, Andy was half in love with Bogey herself. Falling in love with an image on a screen for a couple of hours was a nice, safe diversion. She could turn it off with a simple flick of a button.

It was nearly one when she returned to bed. She slept immediately and didn't dream.

When she awoke, it was midmorning. She stretched lazily and rolled over on her back. She gazed at the bars of sunlight that sliced through the room and were pooled in bright patches on the gold carpet. Her mind was still a bit fuzzy. What day was it?

Sunday. She turned on her side and looked at the clock. Five of ten. She'd slept too late to take the boys to Sunday school. Well, maybe they could make it for worship services. She stretched again, rubbed her eyes and crawled out of bed. In the bathroom she washed her face, then padded barefoot to the kitchen to put on a pot of coffee.

A piece of lined paper torn from a spiral notebook lay in the middle of the kitchen table. She read the note, written in Bo's cramped scrawl:

You were sleeping so hard, I didn't want to disturb you. I'm taking the boys to church. Don't worry about lunch. We'll get something in town. You deserve a day off. Pop

Bo had let himself into the house, looked in on her, found the boys something to wear, left this note and she'd heard nothing. She must've been sleeping like the dead.

Now she could laze about for the rest of the morning. The idea appealed to her. She rarely had such an opportunity. She threw on a cotton duster and brought in the thick Sunday edition of the Omaha newspaper. She lingered over it for an hour, munching on toast spread with plum jam and drinking several cups of coffee.

By noon she'd showered, donned jeans and a knit shirt, and put a load of towels in the washer. She straightened up the house and waited for the boys to come home. One o'clock came and went, and then two. She kept going to the door, expecting to see Bo's old Ford pickup rattling down the street. The minister was sometimes long-winded, but she'd never known him to hold the congregation past twelve-thirty. It shouldn't have taken them more than a half hour to have lunch, so where were they?

She wasn't worried exactly. She could depend on her father to keep an eye on Brad and Tony. It was just that she couldn't imagine what could be keeping them on a Sunday afternoon when most of the town's businesses, including the domino parlor, were closed.

When she ran out of things to do in the house, she found that she had too much time to think. And her thoughts kept going back to last night and Joe. In the end, she was reduced to mopping the kitchen floor, a chore she detested above all others.

It was three o'clock when the boys finally came home. Their white shirts were stained and wrinkled and hanging out of their dress trousers, and their Sunday shoes were scuffed. Nothing that a little soap and water and shoe polish wouldn't fix, but by that time she was so tense she overreacted.

"What happened to your clothes? You look like a couple of urchins!"

Both boys looked down at themselves as though their disheveled state was news to them. Brad began unbuttoning his shirt as he walked through the living room. Tony fell on the couch and reached for the television's remote control.

"Leave that off until you've changed," Andy said crossly. She pointed him toward his bedroom.

"Mom," Brad called from his room across the hall, "guess who we had lunch with."

Andy walked down the hall to stand in Brad's doorway. "Your grandfather. He left me a note."

Brad pulled on a pair of jeans. "Grandpa was with us, but somebody else was there, too." He rummaged in a drawer for a shirt. "Guess who."

Andy sighed, "Brad, I'm not in the mood for guessing games. And you still haven't explained why your clothes are in such a state."

"We played catch in the park," Tony yelled from his room.

"Okay," Brad said, sounding resigned, "if you won't guess, I'll tell you. It was Joe Underwood."

Andy tucked her fingers into the hip pockets of her jeans and asked casually, "How did that happen?"

Brad grabbed his high-top tennis shoes out of the closet and sat on the bed to put them on. "He came into the restaurant while we were eating lunch, so Grandpa asked him to sit with us."

Tony came out of his room in shorts and a T-shirt. "After lunch, we went to the park, and Joe played catch with us."

"What was your grandfather doing?"

"He sat on a park bench and read a contest magazine," Brad said.

"Yeah, and after that we went to the drugstore and Joe bought us all ice cream cones. Double dip," Tony said. "He's really neat, Mom. I like him."

Andy leaned one shoulder against the door of Brad's room, wondering why the boy's eager talk made her feel faintly annoyed. "Had Joe been to church or something?"

"Naw." Brad finished tying his shoelaces. "He said he'd been working in his office all morning." He looked up at Andy. "Did you have a good time with him last night?"

Good would hardly cover it, Andy thought. "It was all right. Did he—did Joe say anything about it?"

"About what?" Brad asked.

Andy tried for a nonchalant shrug. "Oh, dinner last night—or me, or anything."

"No, I don't think he mentioned you at all. Did he, Tony?"

"Nope."

Andy knew that it was stupid to feel irritated, but she did. Obviously she'd made very little impression on Joe. Otherwise, wouldn't it have been natural for him to pump the boys for information about her? Of course, if he had, she'd have been irritated by that, too. He was damned if he asked, and damned if he didn't. Anyway, she had decided to forget about Joe. It was perverse to be disappointed because he hadn't mentioned her name.

"He and Grandpa talked about the TV commercial for a little while," Tony said helpfully, "and the rest of the time Joe played catch with us and took us to the drugstore."

"He said he'd try to come to my ball game Wednesday afternoon," Brad said, "if he gets his work caught up in time."

"Yeah," Tony chimed in, "and he's gonna come to my game next week."

"I imagine Joe's job is very demanding," Andy cautioned. "I wouldn't count on his being able to take off in the middle of the day if I were you."

Tony looked alarmed. "He promised he'd try real hard!"

"He did, Mom," Brad agreed.

"All I'm saying is don't get your hopes up, in case he can't make it."

Tony scowled up at her. "Why are you trying to make us feel bad?"

"I'm not, honey. I—"

"You're just mad 'cause we got our clothes dirty."

"Tony, that's not true."

Tony pushed his bottom lip out. "You always have to work when we have ball games, and you never play catch with us, either. You're no fun!" He stomped into his bedroom and threw himself on his bed.

What had she said to bring this on? Andy wondered as she followed Tony to his room. "Tony?" He pulled the spread up over his head. When Tony was in one of his sulks, ignoring him was usually the best way to handle it, but this time Andy was tempted to paddle him. She felt maligned and wronged. She turned on her heel. "Brad, I'm going over to Pop's. Both of you put your dirty clothes in the hamper. I'll be back shortly."

Bo's front door stood open. When she knocked on the screen door, he called to her from the kitchen. "Who's there?"

"It's me, Pop."

"Come on in."

She found him at the kitchen table, spiral notebook and pencil in hand, with wadded pages from the notebook strewn around him. "Give me some good reasons for using Pinetree dishwasher detergent," he said without looking up.

"You don't have a dishwasher, Pop."

He scratched his head with the eraser end of his pencil. "I know, but I will if I win this contest. Listen to this. 'Pinetree makes my old dishes sparkle like fine bone china, and I love the clean pine-forest smell it gives my whole kitchen.''' He looked up. "That's just twenty-three words. I could use fifty."

Andy dropped into a chair. "You washed your collection of two hundred cups and saucers in the dishwasher, and they make every room in your house sparkle. Your friends think you have a maid."

"Not bad. Except the collection is imaginary."

"Like the dishwasher," Andy pointed out.

Bo nodded and made a note, then gnawed his eraser. "Any other thoughts?"

"Not at the moment," Andy sighed. "Right now I'm put out with Tony. I came over here to cool off."

Bo put his pad and pencil down and propped his elbows on the table. "What'd he do?"

Andy rose and wandered aimlessly to the sink. "Oh, Pop, he didn't do anything. It's what he said. I know I shouldn't let a ten-year-old's temper get under my skin, but it's so unfair."

"Calm down, honey, and tell me what that little pistol said."

Andy paced the room. "He said I never go to his ball games or play catch with him."

"He's pushing your Mom button, kiddo."

She raked both hands through her hair. "I've told him and told him that I get paid by the hour. I can't take off whenever I feel like it."

"Now, Andy, Tony's always cross when he's tuckered out. He had quite an afternoon."

Andy rounded on him. "That's another thing. What the hell is Joe Underwood up to? Doesn't he have anything better to do than hang out in the park with my kids?''

Bo chuckled. ''Andy, you sound like you think Joe's some kind of pervert.''

''I didn't say that!''

''Well, I should hope not. He's a good man. He had as much fun in the park as Brad and Tony did. He told me he hadn't taken time off to relax in so long he'd forgotten what it felt like.'' Bo shook his head. ''Made me feel kinda sorry for him.''

''Somehow I think the last thing Joe needs is sympathy.''

Bo seemed not to have heard the sarcasm in her tone. ''He ought to have a houseful of kids. He knows how to relate to them. He likes 'em.''

''Spare me, Pop. I've already heard what a fantastic guy Joe is from Brad and Tony.''

Bo frowned. ''I don't know what you're so worked up about.'' He studied her thoughtfully. ''You wouldn't be just a teeny bit jealous, would you?''

''No, it's not that.'' She walked back to the table and lowered herself to a chair. ''Pop, I'm working my tail off to support the kids and me. I've had one new dress in the past three years. I'm buying presents I can't afford so Tony won't know that Harley couldn't even be bothered to send a card for his birthday! And what thanks do I get? I'm no fun! Tony said that, can you believe it?''

''He's a child, Andy.''

''I know. Lord, I'm having a pity party, aren't I?'' Impatiently she pushed her hair back from her brow.

"I don't like myself much when I get like this. Whoever said life was fair, huh?"

"Whoever said you have to be a martyr? If you want a new dress, you can buy one without taking food out of your children's mouths. As for buying presents you can't afford, that's a decision you made for yourself. You can stop taking on other people's responsibilities any time you make up your mind to."

"I came over here to get cheered up," she said dryly.

"I thought having the day to yourself would cheer you up, but it seems to have depressed you. It can't be only what Tony said. Are you upset over last night— something Joe said or did that you didn't like?"

On the contrary, she'd liked everything about last night too well. Suddenly she realized that at an unconscious level she'd been listening for her phone to ring all day. She'd expected to hear from Joe. The fact that she'd decided not to get involved with him had nothing to do with it. She was woman enough to want Joe to want to talk to her after that kiss on the porch.

We might as well find out and forget it, he'd said. Maybe it really was that easy for him. While she'd been waiting restlessly for the phone to ring, Joe had been working in his office and playing catch with Brad and Tony. He hadn't even mentioned her name.

"No, Pop," she said with a faint smile. "He was a gentleman."

Bo nodded. "Are you going out with him again?"

"I don't think so."

"Why?"

"For one thing, he hasn't asked me. For another, I can't raise two kids, hold down a job and deal with—with somebody like Joe, too."

"What do you mean—what is Joe like?"

"It's hard to explain, Pop. He seems so—so intense about things. Single-minded. Ambitious—you said he told you he works so hard he rarely has time to relax." And he's still in love with his dead wife, she added silently.

"What's wrong with ambition? Seems to me one of your complaints about Harley was that he never stayed with a job long enough to get promoted. Before you criticize Joe, you'd better take a look at yourself. Did you ever think that Tony might have a point?"

"What do you mean?"

"Maybe you have forgotten how to have fun, Andy."

"Well," she said lightly, getting up, "I don't seem to be getting any sympathy around here. Evidently you've used it all up on Joe. I'm going home."

Andy was glad she had to go to work the next morning. She had no desire to go through two days, back-to-back, with so much time on her hands and too many troubling thoughts intruding on her mind.

At seven-thirty, she stopped by the home of the president of Neptune's First National Bank to leave wallpaper and paint samples. The banker's wife, Nelda Fabian, wanted Andy to redo four rooms in her rambling ranch house.

She should finish the job at the Wilburns' by mid-afternoon, at which time she'd return to consult with

Nelda Fabian about her choices. Andy reached the Wilburn house at ten of eight. She couldn't help noticing as she passed Joe's house that his car was still in the drive.

She'd unloaded her equipment and was stirring a new can of paint when, from the corner of her eye, she saw Joe's car coming down the street. He pulled over to the curb, got out and walked toward her.

Had he been waiting for her to get there before he left the house? She brushed the question aside, telling herself that she was grasping at straws. Pathetic. She kept stirring the paint.

"Good morning, Andy."

She looked up, squinting. The sun sat on his right shoulder. Standing, she tugged the bill of her cap lower over her eyes. "Oh, hi, Joe."

"Am I interrupting?"

She shrugged. "As you can see, I haven't really started yet."

He lit a cigarette and gazed at her as he drew on it. "I enjoyed Saturday evening," he said finally.

What was she supposed to say to that? "Thank you."

"I'd almost forgotten how nice it can be," he said, "being with an attractive woman. I haven't had any social life to speak of since—" He broke off and took another drag on the cigarette.

"Since you lost your wife," Andy finished for him.

"Since before then, actually."

What the hell was he trying to say? Andy wondered. She always had the feeling, no matter what he said to her, that there was much more in his mind than what he put into words. It was all too complicated to try to untangle on a bright June morning when her work was waiting.

"I enjoyed it, too."

"All of it?" he asked quietly.

She knew what he meant, and she wasn't going to be sucked into saying something she'd regret. If he really didn't know how that kiss had affected her, so much the better. "I enjoyed it. Period. No hidden meanings." She didn't wait for him to respond. "Brad and Tony said they saw you in town yesterday."

"I hope the roughhousing didn't ruin their Sunday clothes."

Her brows knit. "The clothes are washable. Actually, though, there's something else I'd like to talk to you about. Brad mentioned that you'd promised to come to his ball game Wednesday afternoon. And Tony says you'll be at his game next week. Both games are in the middle of the afternoon. Did you know that?"

Half annoyed at her attitude, he looked down at her and found himself wondering if her mouth would taste the same this morning as it had Saturday night. "They told me," he said shortly. "I may have to juggle a meeting or two, nothing major. Is there some problem with my planning to go to the boys' ball games?"

She gave him a frankly dubious look. "No, not if you go. But I'd appreciate it if you wouldn't make promises to them that you might not be able to keep. They get enough of that from their father. I don't see Harley changing in the foreseeable future, but at least

I can try to keep other people from hurting them. And you could hurt them because they like you a lot.''

He dropped his cigarette and ground it beneath his shoe. ''Do you find that difficult to understand?''

''I didn't say that,'' she said sharply. ''I'm telling you, don't make any rash promises that may be too much trouble to keep later. What may seem trivial to you can be immensely important to two boys who don't see their father often enough.''

His look was contemplative and not altogether friendly. ''I fully intend to keep any promises I make to Brad and Tony.'' He reached into his pocket for another cigarette. ''He really did a number on you, didn't he?''

She stiffened. ''Who?'' But she knew what he meant.

''Your ex-husband.''

''Harley's not perfect,'' she said grudgingly, ''but I try to make allowances for the boys' sake.''

''Does Harley make allowances for you? Or don't you have any faults?''

''I didn't say that!''

''No, and it's a good thing, because you are carrying around a load of resentment against Harley and, I suspect, it spills out on others. You're as defensive as hell with men, Andy. Did you know that?''

''Oh, really,'' she said frostily.

''Yes, really.''

''Did it ever occur to you that it might not be men I don't like—it might just be you.''

He half smiled, as though she'd said something mildly funny. "No, it didn't occur to me. Not after Saturday night."

"Well, maybe it's because of Saturday night."

He shook his head. "All men aren't like Harley, and if you weren't so stubborn you'd admit it. Lighten up, Andy."

Andy's temper flared hot in an instant. His words were too close to Tony's accusations. Lighten up—you're no fun. Where did he get off, criticizing her? He didn't know anything about her!

"Put a little fun in my life, you mean?" she asked with forced calmness, but she didn't wait for an answer. "Let me tell you something, Joe. My marriage was one long funfest. We traveled! Boy, did we travel. I dragged the boys over ten states, trying to keep up with Harley and his harebrained money-making schemes. Our bills were always just a little more—sometimes a lot more—than Harley's income. Playing hide-and-seek with bill collectors was our favorite sport. Exciting, right? Living on the financial edge didn't faze Harley. He simply didn't think about it—that was my job—and besides there was always that big killing he was going to make tomorrow or next week."

He was watching her with his head cocked to one side. She went on, "I stayed with him a lot longer than I should have because of the boys. But finally, I really couldn't stand it any longer. I had to leave. So maybe I am a little grim and defensive at times. The point is that I don't need somebody who doesn't know the first thing about my life pointing out my faults."

He looked at her for a long moment. Finally he took the cigarette from his mouth. "Holding grudges will make you sick and old before your time."

"I'll outlive you if you keep smoking those things," she shot back. "Now, you must excuse me. I have work to do."

She turned her back on him and poured paint from the can into a clean plastic bucket. She felt his gaze on her for an instant, and then she heard him walk away, get into his car and drive off.

Well, she didn't care! She climbed up the ladder and wielded the brush with quick, angry strokes. Nothing like vigorous physical activity to calm yourself down, she reflected. She finished painting the house at a feverish pace, and by one, she'd put the final touches on the shutters.

As she worked, she kept reminding herself that she really didn't care. She didn't care how rude she'd been to Joe. She didn't care how angry it had made him.

She packed up her gear and went to lunch, feeling worn out and drained.

Chapter Four

Andy tried to stay angry with Joe, yet she couldn't get his words out of her mind.

You're as defensive as hell with men, Andy.

Lighten up, Andy.

She heard Joe's accusations in her mind all afternoon. It didn't help matters that her own father had suggested she'd forgotten how to have fun. She couldn't be angry with Bo, because he loved her and wanted only what was best for her. Furthermore he was the most honest person she knew.

Maybe there was an element of truth in what they were all saying—Tony, her father, Joe. To compensate for Harley's unreliability, had she become too grimly responsible?

As she thought back over the past few weeks, she realized that Brad hadn't even asked her to come to his ball games. More mature and less willing to rock the boat than Tony, her older son had known she'd counter with her "responsibilities" as the family breadwinner. Maybe he understood her justifications better than Tony, or maybe he had simply chosen to keep his own feelings to himself to avoid unpleasantness. He'd done that when she'd told the boys that she was leaving their father and taking them to Neptune to live. Tony, on the other hand, had refused to talk to her for days. In Tony's mind, since she was the one who was leaving, she was to blame for the breakup. At least she had assumed this was Tony's conclusion. He hadn't said it in so many words, but his actions had been loud and clear.

You're as defensive as hell with men, Andy.

Was it possible that she was defensive with her own children as well? After all, how much would it cost her to take a couple of hours off work once in a while to be in the bleachers when Brad or Tony's team played a home game? She could make up for some of the time lost by occasionally starting work at seven in the morning instead of eight. Wasn't one of the perks in being your own boss an ability to set your hours to suit yourself?

She didn't share her thoughts with anyone, but by Wednesday she'd decided to stop work early and go to Brad's ball game in the city park.

She skipped lunch and rushed home at two-thirty to change into shorts and a knit shirt. On her way to the game, she stopped at the drive-in window of a fast-food restaurant for a cold drink and a bag of peanuts. She parked the van in the shade of an elm tree and got out, carrying the food.

The audience was small. About two dozen people were scattered over the home side bleachers. Most parents couldn't take off work at will. Andy scanned the bleachers and found Bo, Tony and Joe in the middle section about five rows up. Brad's team was at bat, and the home side fans were cheering a player who'd just reached first base safely.

She climbed the steps and sat down beside Tony. "Hey, sport, mind if I sit here?"

Tony darted a look at her that was first surprised, then delighted. "Mom! What're you doing here? Don't you have to work?"

"Somebody recently told me I'm no fun, so I decided to play hooky." She held the bag of peanuts toward him, and he took a handful of the still-warm nuts and started to shell them. "What's the score?"

"Three to two. The other team is ahead."

Joe, who was sitting on the other side of Tony, had been looking at her with a glimmer of approval in his gray eyes. "Glad you could work us into your schedule, Mom." He was wearing faded jeans and an old sweatshirt with the arms cut off of it. A red cap with a bill was pulled down on his forehead. Leaving the office in midafternoon had felt odd, but he was enjoying himself.

She sent him a sidelong look and thrust her sack at him. "Stuff a peanut in your mouth, Underwood."

The corner of Joe's mouth lifted as he poked his hand into the sack. "Since you ask so politely, I'll have several. Thanks."

"Hey, leave some, will you," she yelped rudely. "This is my lunch."

Quirking an eyebrow at her, Joe shelled a peanut and popped it into his mouth.

"Want some, Pop?"

"Not now, Andy." Bo had given her a distracted wave as she sat down, then returned his attention to the field. He sat on the edge of his seat, intent on the game. "One more strike, and they're out."

"What's the inning?" she asked.

"Four," Tony said.

"I thought the game was supposed to start at three."

"Both teams were here and raring to go," Joe said, "so they didn't wait. I only got here ten minutes ago myself. As promised."

Ignoring his barb, Andy leaned forward and rested her elbows on her bare knees. She shook her Styrofoam cup, rattling the ice cubes, and drew on the straw. She admitted to herself that she was surprised that Joe had come, in spite of what he'd told her Monday morning. Why had he? Walking away from work in the middle of the afternoon didn't fit in with the ambition she knew was a strong part of his personality. From what he'd told Bo Sunday, he was in the habit of putting his job first. He even went to the office on Sunday morning. So why had he juggled meetings to spend the afternoon in the sweltering heat, watching two Little League teams, for a boy he barely knew? Who was Joe Underwood, anyway?

She watched a towheaded youngster take a lunging swipe at the ball and miss by a foot. She groaned as

Tony ripped his ball cap off and slapped it against his leg in disappointment. Brad's team ran out on the field. Brad was playing second base.

"Andy, I didn't see you at the Wilburn house this morning," Joe said idly, his eyes on the pitcher, who was warming up.

"I finished there. I'm working for the Fabians on Tenth Street now."

Joe glanced at her with frank interest. He hadn't been able to admit it to himself before, but he'd left his house after eight the last two mornings, hoping to catch sight of her, and all the time, she'd been across town on Tenth. It appeared he might as well go back to his old habit of getting to the office before anybody else. Especially if he was going to take off early again next week to attend Tony's game. Actually, he'd been startled to hear himself promising the boy he'd be there. But once he'd promised, he'd had to keep his word—for cautious, defensive Andy as much as for Brad and Tony.

He liked the way the sunlight shot her hair through with red-gold streaks. She had a stunning face with delicate angles, a few golden freckles and soft skin. The way she had of holding herself a little apart both annoyed and tantalized him. He sensed that there was a wide streak of earthy sexuality running deep in her, perhaps so deep that she didn't even know it was there. At the thought, his gaze was drawn downward. The knit shirt fit like a second skin, emphasizing the curve of her breasts, then hugging her slender waist. His glance followed the line of her body to the long, tanned legs. He knew they would be warm and silky smooth to the touch, and he wanted to touch them.

When Andy felt his gaze leave her to return to the field, she turned her head to look at him. He hadn't disappointed Brad, so she couldn't be annoyed with him for acting so at-home with her father and Tony. Yet she didn't understand him. He'd taken such a quick interest in her boys, and she couldn't help wondering about his motives. Bo had said he liked kids. Okay, she'd accept that—for now. He was friendly and considerate with Tony and Brad. His attitude toward her was sometimes friendly, too. At other times it was something else. Well, she already knew he was complicated.

What kind of lover would he be? Not casual, she knew instinctively. It was in his eyes—those smoky, deep-set eyes. Should she ever want to become involved with a man, Joe Underwood would definitely not be a wise choice. He felt things too intensely, and somehow she knew he'd make her plumb the depths of her own emotions. He'd overwhelm her—she could lose her way back to the simple, structured existence she'd built so painstakingly since her divorce. She had to remind herself that she preferred easy, comfortable relationships like the one she'd had with Harley in the early days.

She forced her attention back to the field. The game continued to be a close one. In the seventh, Brad hit a spectacular home run. Unfortunately there was nobody else on base when he did it, and in the end Brad's team lost by two points.

They waited for him at the edge of the playing field. He came toward them, dirty and sweaty, kicking dirt with every step, his shoulders slumped and his head bowed in disappointment.

"Nice homer," Bo said, but Brad didn't even look up.

Andy put her arm around him. "Good game, Brad."

"No, it wasn't," Brad complained. "We lost."

"You got a hit every time you went to bat," Joe said. "Don't be so hard on yourself."

Brad looked up at him unhappily. "We had to lose with you and Mom watching."

"Your mom and I have lost a few things in our lives, too," Joe said. Andy looked up sharply, wondering what he meant. He went on in the same reasonable tone, "You played well, Brad. You gave it your best shot. That's all anybody can do."

Tony, as well as Brad, was looking at Joe warily. They hadn't expected so much understanding. Harley would have reeled off a list of mistakes Brad and his teammates had made. Harley's philosophy was, Show me a good loser, and I'll show you a loser. He'd have hammered away at Brad's ego for the rest of the day, always reminding Brad that he merely wanted to help him improve so that next time he'd be a winner. Harley would actually have believed he had Brad's best interests at heart. He might even have apologized later for going a bit overboard, but the damage would have been done. Harley's intense emotional involvement in the boy's sports events had been but one of the many aspects of her ex-husband's personality that Andy hadn't known how to deal with. As a teenager, Harley had wanted to be a pro baseball player, but he hadn't been good enough. He'd started trying to "do it over" through his sons almost as soon as they were walking.

Losing today's game meant that Brad's team probably wouldn't make it to the league play-offs, and it was obvious that he didn't quite know how to take Joe's commonsense attitude. Andy knew he expected it from Bo, but grandfathers were supposed to let you get away with murder.

"Joe's right," Andy said, giving him a grateful glance over Brad's head. "You were good, Brad. So let's don't replay the game for the rest of the day. Okay?"

"I have something a lot more fun in mind, anyway," Joe said. "Let's go to town and stuff ourselves with hamburgers and fries. I'll pay. You feel up to it, Brad?"

"I guess so."

"Me, too!" Tony chimed in.

Joe looked at Bo and then Andy. "Okay with everybody?"

"Beats cooking dinner," Bo said.

Andy shrugged. She couldn't be the lone dissenter. Tony would accuse her of being no fun again. "Why not?" she agreed.

At Dot's Café on Main Street, they ordered burger baskets and malts. Joe and the boys sat on one side of the booth, Bo and Andy on the other. Joe's watchful gaze was on her whenever she looked his way. She managed to focus on food when her basket was set in front of her. She took a big bite of her burger, sighed, "yummm," drenched her potatoes in ketchup, then nibbled on a French fry. Even Brad was attacking his food with gusto, his disappointment receding quickly.

"This," said Andy, stuffing another French fry into her mouth, "may be the best idea you ever had, Joe."

He gave her a rakish look. "You haven't heard all of my ideas."

She grinned at him. Surrounded by her family, she felt safe. "I don't think I want to, either."

Bo looked at them curiously, then quickly dropped his eyes to his food. He made an elaborate ritual of rearranging the layers of his burger and adding salt and pepper.

Joe finished first and lit a cigarette. Andy popped her last French fry into her mouth and drained the final drops of her strawberry malt. Joe had been listening to Bo talk about the latest contests he'd entered and he seemed to feel as at-home with Andy's family as he would in a corporate boardroom. She was lulled into letting down her guard.

"Pop," she said casually, "why don't you and the boys take the van home? I need to talk to Joe about something."

"I wanna ride with Joe," Tony protested.

Joe snagged Andy's gaze and held it. "You go along with your grandfather, Tony. I'll bring your mother home later."

"Aw," Tony whined.

"Don't be a baby," Brad grumbled.

"Who's a baby!"

Bo rose abruptly. "Come on, Tony. I want to go by the post office. You take your time, Andy." He herded the boys out of the café, Tony still complaining about wanting to go in Joe's car, and Brad rolling his eyes in gross disgust at such juvenile behavior.

Andy leaned her elbows on the table and watched Joe put out his cigarette. "You should give those things up, you know."

He settled his cap on his head and grinned at her. "Don't you have any vices?"

She pursed her lips and pretended to consider the question. She shook her head. "Nope, can't think of a single one." She laughed suddenly. "Would you call that a vice within itself?"

"Maybe," he drawled lazily. "If I believed it."

She spread her hand on her breast and sighed, "I'm crushed."

The skin at the outer corners of his eyes crinkled charmingly. "Don't be. Totally virtuous people are usually boring. You're not boring, Andy."

"Thank you kindly, sir," she said with exaggerated gravity, then flashed a teasing grin. "I still think you should give up those coffin nails."

Joe moved his shoulders. "I'll take it under advisement."

"Good. Every chance I get, I'll remind you."

He gave her a long, steady look. She couldn't decipher its meaning. "Ready to go?"

"Sure."

He paid the check, and they went out to the car. He turned the air conditioner on full blast. She angled an air vent to hit her face and settled back against the warm leather. "I wanted to tell you—" she began.

"Not now," he cut her off. "Wait till we get to my place."

She sat up straight as he turned a corner and took a street that led away from her house. "I didn't say I'd go to your place! I told Pop I'd be home soon!"

"And he told you not to hurry," he said easily. "You can take time enough for one glass of wine, can't you?"

"I—I don't know. I hadn't thought about it. I only wanted to—"

"Talk. We'll get to that." His voice was calm, almost remote. "Try to relax, Andy. You took the afternoon off, remember?"

She thought about it a moment. A glass of wine would be nice. Besides, she was curious about where he lived. She glanced over at him. Okay, she was more curious about Joe than about his house. A little wine, a little talk. If he had an idea that it might progress to something else, she'd set him straight. Anyway, he'd given her no reason to believe he had any such idea. No reason for alarm. She could handle it. "I guess I can spare another half hour."

He didn't reply. Soon they were turning into his driveway. She followed him through the door, looking around with open curiosity. The house was cool and dim because the venetian blinds were closed. As her eyes got used to the dimness, she saw that the rooms were perfectly clean and neat. No books, newspapers or magazines lying about, no dirty dishes in the sink. When he opened the refrigerator, she saw a bottle of white wine, a half-gallon milk carton and two apples. Nothing else.

Joe removed the wine from the refrigerator, eased the cork out and got two stemmed glasses from the cabinet. He poured the wine and handed her a glass.

She sipped slowly, trailing one hand over the shining Formica cabinet top. She leaned back against the counter. "You don't spend much time here, do you?"

His glance raked the bare walls of the kitchen. "It shows, I guess."

"Yeah, it doesn't have a lived-in look. Don't you even take a newspaper?"

He shrugged and sipped his wine. "I get it at the office. I spend most of my waking hours at the plant. You're my first guest."

"I suppose I should be honored." She avoided his contemplative gaze.

"Would you like to sit down?" He gestured toward the kitchen doorway.

She nodded and walked into the adjoining living room. Narrow shafts of sunlight coming from between the partially closed slats of the venetian blinds were reflected on the ceiling. A large still life of fruit in a wooden bowl was the only thing on the living-room wall. The furniture was upholstered in uninspired blues and browns. Joe had obviously rented the house furnished. An ashtray and two photographs in a hinged, silver, double frame sat on a lamp table. The photographs were angled so that, from across the room, Andy couldn't see them clearly.

She curled into a corner of the blue tweed couch and watched Joe settle into the other corner, one arm stretched out along the couch back. His fingers brushed her shoulder lightly. "I wanted to apologize," she said, "for being so irritable with you Monday morning, and for thinking you'd made promises to the boys you wouldn't keep. The accusations were unfounded. I overreacted, and I'm sorry."

"I understood where you were coming from," he said. "Unfortunately you were generalizing from a single case, your ex-husband."

She nodded, accepting the assessment. "Yes, you're right. I wasn't being very logical or fair."

His look was considering. "I think I know enough about you now to know there was another reason for your reaction. You're a classic rescuer, Andy."

Her fingers tightened on the stem of her glass. "What do you mean by that?"

Slowly Joe drained his glass and bent to set it on the coffee table. He leaned back. His fingers lightly caressed the curve of her shoulder. "Do you really want me to elaborate?"

She frowned, sensing criticism. "You started it, you'd better finish it."

"Okay. You rescue Harley by buying gifts and putting his name on them. I'd bet money that you spent most of your marriage running around trying to fix the unpleasant consequences of his irresponsibility."

Her eyes widened in surprise. How did he know that? And why must he always put her on the defensive? "I had—have my reasons, which I shouldn't have to explain to you. Honestly! I thought we could have a pleasant conversation..."

"Why do you do it, Andy? Are you still in love with him?"

"Harley?" She laughed, but there was no humor in the sound. "I don't even like him very much. I can't imagine what I ever saw in him."

"Then why do you keep pulling his fat out of the fire?"

"It has nothing to do with Harley," she protested. "I'm protecting my children."

"Rescuing them from disappointment, to put it another way," he said quietly. "You can't protect them all their lives, Andy, no matter how much you want to."

It was what Bo had told her more than once. For an instant she saw a dark flash of pain in Joe's expression, and then it was over. His eyes were calm again, and the fingers curved on her shoulder relaxed.

Restless, she got rid of her glass and pushed herself up from the couch. "They'll find out about their father soon enough," she murmured and wandered across the room. "I don't expect you to understand. You don't have children." Idly, she lifted the silver frame from the lamp table and turned it for a better light. The photographs were of a boy and a girl, about eight and six years old. They had dark curly hair and blue eyes.

"Who are they?" she asked over her shoulder, returning the photographs to the table. "Relatives of yours?" She turned around.

He levered himself from the couch. A look had come into his eyes that she didn't understand. For an instant she was caught in confusion, in the dark tragedy she'd sensed in him before, a tragedy that she knew nothing about. "Yeah," he said briefly and, as though he needed something to do, swept up their empty glasses and took them to the kitchen.

Andy followed hesitantly. He'd opened the blinds over the sink and was standing, staring out at the backyard. "Joe? I'm sorry if I touched a nerve." When he didn't move or respond in any way, she took a deep breath and let it out. Why had he told her he had no children? "They're your children." Of course they were his children. The little boy looked so like him she would have to be blind not to see it. Still he said nothing. "When I said that you didn't understand, I had no idea." He'd told her that his wife was dead. Why weren't the children with him? "Do they live with their grandparents?"

"No."

Why wouldn't he look at her?

After another tense moment, he turned around. "They're dead," he said in a flat voice. "David and Sarah died with their mother in a plane crash almost two years ago."

The words, delivered in a controlled monotone, stabbed her heart. "Oh, Joe." How would she live if she lost Brad and Tony? How would she get up in the morning? Pity flooded through her, overwhelmed her. Without thinking, she ran to him and put her arms around him. She pressed her cheek against his shoulder, wanting to comfort, to share his pain.

His arms came around her and squeezed convulsively. His jaw rested against her forehead, and she felt his breath warm in her hair. After a moment, she asked quietly, "That's why you wanted to come to Neptune, isn't it?"

"Yeah," he murmured. "Everywhere I went in Detroit, there were reminders. Places we'd gone together. I thought it would get easier, but it didn't. So when they decided to open the plant here, I applied for a transfer."

She lifted her head to look into his eyes. "Has it helped?"

He nodded. Her blue eyes overflowed with sympathetic warmth. For an instant, he wanted to tell her everything, but he choked back the words. What would it accomplish? He'd tried. Miriam had tried. There was no one to blame. And yet in the dark hours of the night when he couldn't sleep, he blamed himself. If he hadn't suggested to Miriam that she take the children to visit her parents, they wouldn't have been on that plane.

Miriam. He had no photographs of her in the house. There were times when he could hardly remember what she'd looked like. Yet he'd known Andy only a short time and he had memorized every angle of her face, every curve of her body. He thought about her too often, imagined ways he'd like to make love to her. And now she was in his arms, looking at him with eyes that threatened to drown him, and the house was so still.

Andy saw the confusion in his eyes, saw when it changed to decision. Her mind was perfectly alert and clear, and she could easily have said something, shifted away, denied the sudden physical urge that gripped her the second after she recognized the same urge in his eyes. She told herself that he needed a woman's warmth and understanding just then, that it would be insensitive to walk out and leave him with his pain.

She couldn't admit that it was the man she was drawn to, not merely a fellow creature who was suffering and needed comfort.

Chapter Five

Joe lowered his mouth to hers. This time the kiss did not begin with light, tentative experimentation as their first kiss had. Now their lips sought each other with more knowledge and with an edge of desperation. His moist, seductive mouth was familiar now, and his taste, touched with the flavor of wine, was just like it had been the first time. A jolt of passion raced through her, and she slid her tongue along his, seeking the feeling of giddiness that his earlier kiss had given her.

Heat spread through her body as quickly as a grass fire after a two-month drought. The depth of her passion bewildered her. She made a small, greedy sound in her throat, begging for more. His hands cupped the back of her tilted head. His fingers, tangled in the thick, auburn mass of her hair, moved convulsively.

She moved against him, wanting the pressure of his chest against her breasts, wanting his lower body crushing hers, wanting to fill the aching void deep inside her.

The need that had erupted in her was confusing, yet she recognized it as the primitive, shuddering need of a woman for a man. It went deeper than any she'd ever known before. She felt an answering shudder run through his body, but he continued to touch her only with his mouth and his hands in her hair. Yet the effect was shattering.

The only sound in the house was the faraway hum of the central air-conditioning unit. Andy felt warm sunlight from the kitchen window on her arms, which were wound around Joe's neck. One palm was spread against his upper back, the fingers clenching and unclenching.

Though his fingers dug into her scalp, he was holding back. She could feel the rigidity of fierce control in his torso and arms. While his mouth pillaged hers unmercifully, she pushed her body closer to his. His back was against the countertop, and he couldn't shift away from the pressure. She ran her hand over the taut muscles at the back of his neck and plowed her fingers through his hair.

Her body's eager demands for more stretched Joe's control to the limit. She was in his house, in his arms, as he'd dreamed of her being. The seductive pressure of her body on his made him wonder if he wasn't dreaming now. The first time, she had pulled away from him after a few stunned moments, and she'd made it clear that the distance between them would remain. Today she seemed to be keeping nothing back. Her mouth was wet and giving and eager. Her body was soft and warm and beguiling. Her clean, natural scent filled his nostrils.

She nibbled at his lips and said his name in a throaty whisper that was neither coy nor subtle, but purely, mindlessly sexual. For the first time in two years, the desire to sweep aside restraint and willpower was so strong that it made his mind swim and his body throb uncontrollably. He wanted—needed—to take what she was offering with such sweet ferocity.

But he held on to the tattered shreds of his restraint while he listened to the relentless questions echoing through his churning mind. Why was Andy so different today? What had caused her to reverse her decision about keeping a distance between them? This time she had come to him, come after him. He forced himself to think, to remember how it had started.

Of course.

Andy was trying to make amends for forcing him to tell her about his children. She had thrown her arms around him out of compassion. It was the most natural thing in the world for Andy; she was a rescuer, a nurturer. She wouldn't be such a conscientious mother without that determination to protect those she cared about. He wanted Andy desperately—but not like this.

His thoughts were enough to jolt him back to sanity. When he made love to her, he had to be sure that pity didn't come into it.

With the strongest force of will he'd ever been called on to exert, he dropped his arms and lifted his head. "This is a mistake."

As she looked into his shuttered eyes, Andy's mood was destroyed. Panic rushed in to take its place. What was she doing? How quickly she had forgotten restraint, thrown caution away. The only explanation she could come up with was temporary insanity.

She could see determination and anger in him. Did he imagine she was trying to seduce him? Was he blaming her for his frustrated physical urges? Her own anger bubbled up. She was suffering as much frustration as he. Her heart was hammering, and her legs threatened to give way beneath her. Temper gave her the strength to stay upright and step back.

"You're right," she said shortly. "I don't know what it is about you that makes me forget good sense, but this only proves that I was right the first time. I should keep my distance."

He stiffened. "You made the first move, Andy."

"It was your idea to come here," she shot back. She glanced down at the hand gripping her upper arm. "I wanted to go home."

His fingers tightened their hold briefly, then he flung his hand away as though he'd touched something hot. She was right. He had overridden her objections and brought her here. Since Saturday night, he'd imagined kissing her, again and again. When she'd put her arms around him in sympathy, he'd felt the stirring of sexual desire instantly. He had initiated the kiss.

Calm settled on him. "Let's just say we're both to blame for what happened."

She stared at him for another moment, then nodded. "Fair enough." He had been vulnerable, an emotion that she had created with her careless questions about the photographs. She had told herself she only wanted to comfort him, but was that really true? She suspected that neither of their motives would stand up to close scrutiny.

He stuffed his hands into his jeans' pockets and smiled lopsidedly. "I'll take you home now."

"All right . . ." Andy had a sense of incompleteness about what had happened between them, but she didn't know how to talk about it without sounding as though she wanted to finish it.

They went out to the car, got in and drove down the street in silence. They'd had a very close call, and they both knew it. He was still grieving for his family. The loneliness must be almost overwhelming at times. Now she understood his interest in her boys better than she had before. She hoped he didn't start thinking of them as substitutes for the children he'd lost.

Maybe that was what attracted him to her. The thought brought an ache of disappointment, of regret. She must be careful. She was too easy a mark for Joe because sometimes she suffered from loneliness, too. Lonely people could mistake desperation for something more. What if we'd ended up in Joe's bed? Andy asked herself. How would she be feeling right now? Dismayed, she reflected, because she couldn't see any place for them to go from there.

When they reached Andy's house, Joe cleared his throat. "Andy."

She turned toward him, her hand ready to open the door. "Yes?"

"We..." He cleared his throat once more and flexed his fingers on the wheel. "We could have dinner again."

Her thoughts on the drive home had convinced her that spending another evening with Joe would be a mistake. It would be playing with fire. They were both too vulnerable, and they struck too many sparks off each other.

"I don't think so, Joe." She opened the door and got out. "Thanks for the ride." She turned and ran into the house.

Friday afternoon, as Andy drove down Main Street, she noticed a small crowd of people in front of the domino parlor. Others were crossing the street to join the group. A camera crew had set up equipment on the sidewalk, forcing pedestrians to make a wide circle out to the curb and back. Joe was deep in conversation with one of the cameramen.

Then Andy saw Brad and Tony with two of their friends perched on the hood of Bo's old pickup, which was parked, nose in, at the curb. Bo was in the open doorway of the domino parlor, in striped overalls and a blue chambray shirt. Pulled midway down his forehead was a cap with Friendly Domino Parlor, Neptune, Nebraska, printed across the front.

Andy pulled into the first empty parking space she saw and walked up to the crowd of onlookers. "Hey, Andy!" It was Ed Rankin, his camera hanging around his neck. "Bo's rehearsing for his commercial. Come on up here by me where you can see."

Andy wove her way to the front of the crowd to stand beside Rankin. When she looked Joe's way again, he was staring at her. He stirred and pulled his eyes away.

"Okay! Ready for a trial run, Bo?"

A man at the back of the crowd yelled, "Smile real purty, Bo!"

Bo tucked his thumbs behind the bib of his overalls, pushed his chest out and said "Cheese."

Ed Rankin chortled and snapped Bo's picture.

Bo waved. "Hi, Andy." He looked over at Joe. "You gonna film this?"

"Not this time," Joe said, "so relax. We're just practicing. Go back in the domino parlor and come out again, as though you'd just finished a game."

Bo sauntered inside and, after a few seconds, opened the door and stepped out again. He hesitated and looked to Joe for direction. "You want me to say my lines now?"

"Go ahead," Joe said.

Bo ducked his head, pulled on the bill of his cap and loudly cleared his throat. "I never lived anywhere but Neptune, Nebraska, in my whole life. But I been down to the barn and back—in a manner of speakin'. When NM came out with these new Neptune auto-mo-biles, I liked the name—" he touched his cap "—naturally—but I don't buy cars fer the name. I buy 'em for quality and dependability." Bo ambled toward the curb, then turned back. "That's why I bought me a new Neptune."

A smattering of applause ran through the spectators and from the back came a shrill whistle. Bo beamed. What a ham, Andy thought.

"Did I say it right, Joe?" He was gazing at Joe with the utmost confidence and trust. Andy noticed also that Brad and Tony were watching Joe direct the proceedings with wonder. She felt a flare of resentment. Joe seemed to have won her family's loyalty in a very short time.

"Yeah, but let's try it again. Say it slower this time, Bo."

Bo went back into the domino parlor. He stepped out and said, "I never lived anywhere but Neptune, Nebraska—"

"Slower yet," Joe yelled.

Bo plucked at the bill of his cap and started over with an exaggerated slowness that made his country drawl more pronounced than ever. Joe was nodding, saying, "That's it . . . that's it . . . slow, now."

Bo went through his lines again, more to Joe's satisfaction. He's really getting into the spirit of this, Andy thought with a frown. It annoyed her. Did Bo realize that Joe was making him sound like a hayseed? Bo delivered his lines several more times, his drawl deepening, and each time he received laughter and applause from the watchers.

"You folks get all the horseplay out of your system," Joe told the crowd. "When we film it, we'll have to have complete silence."

The crowd nodded at Joe, rapt. Andy turned away. She'd seen enough. "Excuse me . . . excuse me," she murmured as she made her way back to the street. As she got into the van, she glanced over her shoulder. Brad and Tony didn't even know she had left. Their attention, like everybody else's, was riveted on Joe, who was settling Bo's cap at a more rakish angle.

Andy backed into the street and drove away without looking back again. If she'd stayed any longer, she would have objected to Joe's direction of the commercial. He was making Bo sound like some backwoods hillbilly. People would laugh at the commercial, all right. But they'd be laughing at her father, not with him.

By the time she got home, Andy was seething with righteous indignation. As soon as Bo came in, she'd tell him exactly what Joe was doing, since he couldn't seem to see it for himself. She hated to spoil his fun, but wasn't that better than standing by and watching him being turned into a laughingstock?

She showered and started dinner preparations and waited for Bo and the boys.

"Mom!" Brad called as he and Tony slammed into the house.

"In the kitchen. Wash up. Dinner's ready."

A few minutes later, they sat down at the table. "Why'd you leave so soon?" Tony asked, transferring a large helping of lasagna to his plate.

"I had things to do here," Andy replied. "Why didn't Pop come over for dinner? You remembered to ask him, didn't you?"

"Oh, sure," Brad said between mouthfuls. "He said he was too excited to eat right now."

Great, Andy thought morosely. And here she was, planning to go next door and puncture Bo's fantasy balloon.

"Wasn't Grandpa funny, Mom?" Tony asked.

"Uh-huh," Andy mumbled, thinking that a ten-year-old's idea of humor left a lot to be desired.

"You should've stayed," Brad said. "He got better and better."

Hickier and hickier, Andy would bet. "Next time he's gonna rehearse inside the domino parlor," Tony informed her, "with his friends, playing a game of dominos."

"You should've seen Mr. Rankin," Brad put in. "He was more excited than Grandpa about being in the commercial, and he won't even get to say anything."

Andy closed her eyes briefly. She could just see it. Old man Rankin, Ed's father, with his frayed suspenders holding his pants up over his paunch and leaving two inches of skinny ankles bare. "Always looks like he's expecting a flood," Bo was fond of saying. And Dermas Connolley would be there, too, with his snaggletoothed grin. "Won't get dentures," Bo had told Andy. "Dermas says if God had intended man to mess with nature, he'd have sent us into the world with a supply of spare parts." And Barney Morse chewing on the stub of a cigar. All of them posing for the camera as Bo drawled his lines.

After dinner, she left the boys to clear the table and went next door before she lost her nerve. She didn't want to spoil Bo's fun; she just wanted him to face reality. Bo was watching a boxing match on television. He turned off the sound when Andy came in.

"I saw you watching the rehearsal today," he greeted her. "What'd you think?"

Andy sank into a chair, trying to remember the judicious words with which she'd meant to start. "I—uh . . ."

Bo was still too wound up to wait for her response. He sat forward in his chair and said earnestly, "I been thinking, Andy. If this commercial hits the public's fancy, I could be in demand for more. I could be a star!"

"Oh, Pop—"

"It's not all that unusual. Think of how many older people you see in commercials—all having a second career. Remember the 'Where's the beef?' lady? And that old gal who talks to grapes in that skivvies commercial?" He sat back and let out a deep breath, as though the thought of potential stardom had knocked the breath out of him.

"Those were flukes, Pop. Don't count on—"

"I know. Joe told me there's no way you can predict which commercials will catch on. The public's fickle." He nodded wisely. "They have to run my commercial in a few test markets first, but if it goes nationwide, I could make twenty thousand—or more."

"That would be nice, Pop, but—"

"Of course, it's not the money so much as doing something I get such a kick out of." He shook his head wonderingly. "Joe says I'm a natural, and I never even suspected I had this—this talent in me."

Oh, Lord, Andy moaned silently. She hadn't seen Bo so enthusiastic about anything since his retirement. He enjoyed entering contests, but that was only a hobby—something, she suspected, that Bo viewed as a way to keep his mind active and his spare time filled. He'd won several prizes, but all together they weren't worth what he'd spent on subscriptions and postage. But if this commercial was a success . . .

"I tell you, Andy, that Joe's a smart young man. And just as comfortable and natural as an old shoe. He's gone a long ways in his profession for a man his age—and he's going much farther, mark my word. Some folks would let success like that go to their heads, but not Joe."

As Andy had suspected, Bo had followed Brad and Tony in falling under Joe's spell. She was the only one in the family with any objectivity. But could she tell Bo that his hero was making him look like a boob? She cleared her throat.

"Well, would you listen to me," Bo said, "running on like a freight train and not giving you a chance to get a word in edgewise. Did you want to talk to me about something, Andy?"

"Yes." Andy now remembered how she'd meant to start, but the words were stuck in her throat. Why was she the only one who could see what was happening? Why did she always have to be the voice of reason? She couldn't do it. Even if she could convince Bo she was right, he wouldn't thank her. "I just wanted to tell you there's plenty of lasagna left, if you want some."

He waved a hand, and his gaze wandered to the silent boxing match on the television screen. "Thanks, but I already had a sandwich."

Andy sighed. "Okay, just thought I'd offer. I'd better go back home now." She got up and kissed the top of her father's head. "See you later, Pop."

She felt faintly depressed for the rest of the evening. Maybe she should keep her opinion to herself. After all, nobody had asked for it. The boys went to bed at ten, and she sat trying to read a magazine article about how to decorate whole rooms for less than a hundred dollars. She might be able to use one or two of the ideas when customers on a strict budget asked for her advice.

When a knock sounded at her door at ten forty-five, she thought that Bo must have changed his mind about the lasagna. Or maybe he was still too wound up to sleep and wanted to talk.

She switched on the porch light and had the door half-open before she realized it wasn't Bo at all. It was Joe Underwood. What the hell was he doing on her front porch at this time of night?

She crossed her arms and glared at him through the screen.

He was dressed in shorts, a T-shirt, and running shoes, as though he'd been out jogging, but he wasn't perspiring. A walk then, since Andy hadn't heard a car.

"Did I wake you?"

"No."

He waited a moment. "You look cross, so I thought I must have."

"What do you want, Underwood?"

His look was dry. "You left yourself wide open with that one. But I'll settle for a talk."

"Well, I'm sorry, but all your admirers are asleep. There's only me." Her voice dripped sarcasm, and then she realized that she was a bit ashamed of herself. She knew what her problem was. She'd been stewing for hours over the commercial, yet she hadn't been able to say a word to Bo about it. Now she was spoiling for a fight.

"What the hell is wrong with you?" His voice was sharp, impatient.

Andy opened the door, forcing him to step back. She closed it behind her. "I don't want you to wake the boys." She walked down the front steps, stopping at the bottom and tucking her fingers into the side pockets of her shorts. "You want to know what's wrong with me?" Her voice was low-toned, but angry. "I'll tell you what's wrong with me. I watched your rehearsal today."

"I saw you. If you'd stayed until it was over, I'd have offered to buy you a cold drink."

"I didn't want to stay! I saw more than enough while I was there."

Joe took her arm impatiently and turned her around so that the light from the porch illuminated her face. "Good God, you're furious. You're trembling."

"You sound surprised."

He sighed. "Andy, whatever's bothering you, spit it out."

"Don't play the wide-eyed innocent with me, Joe. I saw that rehearsal. I know what you're doing to Pop."

Damn, what was she so worked up about? And did she have any idea how much he wanted to kiss her angry mouth into soft submission at that moment? "Then maybe you'll enlighten me," he said, trying to remain calm, "because it seems to me that what I'm doing is giving Bo a chance thousands of people would kill for."

She should've known he wouldn't understand. She threw his hand from her arm. "You're making him look like a hillbilly moron! He'll be a laughing-stock!"

Joe stared at her, flabbergasted. Did she believe what she was saying? "My God, woman, Bo is having the time of his life. Where's your sense of humor?"

She met his look for a tense instant, then stomped into the darkness of the yard. She halted beside the cracked stone birdbath that a former renter had left behind. Since it would no longer hold water, Andy used it as a stand for a wooden planter filled with hot-pink petunias. She braced her hands on the rim of the stone bowl and felt her anger leaving as quickly as it had come. She heard Joe's muffled footsteps in the grass as he came to stand behind her.

"Andy, I could tell you were upset about something at the rehearsal today. That's why I wanted to talk to you. But I had no idea—" He broke off in frustration and ran his fingers through his hair to keep from grabbing her again. "I can't believe this," he said helplessly. "Bo is playing a role. It has nothing to do with him personally. You haven't told him how you feel, have you?" His voice sharpened on the question.

"No, of course not." She bowed her head until the petunias' velvet blossoms brushed her nose. She smelled the rich, damp scent of the soil and the barely discernible fragrance of the flowers. Joe was right. She'd known all along that she was overreacting again, but she'd been hiding it from herself so that she could stay mad at Joe. What was wrong with her? Was she turning into a humorless shrew? Once she'd been a cheerful woman, but then the boys had come along, and motherhood had forced her to take her responsibilities seriously. She'd had to stop kidding herself about Harley, telling herself that any day he'd "find himself" and settle down. She'd had to accept the fact that Harley wasn't likely to change and that she'd fallen in love with the man she'd imagined he could be with the support of "a good woman," and not with the man he was.

Now she blamed herself for being so gullible and tried to assuage her guilt by protecting the boys from the truth about their father. Joe was probably right about that, too, damn him.

And today she'd come very close to hurting Bo's feelings when she raced to his rescue. Andy on a white charger, she thought miserably. In Bo's case, it was laughable—at least she'd probably laugh once she'd had more time to think about it. Her father still had all his faculties, and he was as independent as a hog on ice. The last thing Bo wanted or needed was for his daughter to explain the facts of life to him. He was nobody's fool.

"Andy?"

Sighing, she lifted her head and turned around. He was standing so close to her that she could feel his warm breath on her forehead and smell his scent. "Look, I was tired and maybe I was too quick to judge."

His hand clasped her arm loosely. His thumb skimmed over the inside of her elbow, and her pulse speeded up. "This isn't about Bo at all, is it? It's about us, what we feel when we're together."

"Perhaps, I . . ." She trailed off as her thoughts got mired in confusion. Nothing had changed. He was a lonely man who missed the family he would be with at this moment if they hadn't died. Whatever he felt when he and Andy were together, a part of it was the fact that her children helped to fill the void in his heart left by the loss of his own. Andy was as convinced of that as ever, and the complications didn't stop there. How much of what she felt was due to her own aching need to have a man in her life again? She didn't know.

"Can't we be honest with each other?" He wanted to kiss her so much that he could taste it.

"I'm not sure what the truth is," she murmured and found that her hands were resting on his shoulders. Her breasts brushed his shirt. Had he moved closer, or had she? Their lips, so close, hesitated, then barely touched. A car rounded the corner and roared down the street, and for a second, they were caught in the beam from the headlights. Youthful voices split the night with catcalls as the car passed. Andy and Joe drew back from each other with a jerk.

Suddenly self-conscious, Andy linked her hands behind her back. "Well..."

Reaching out, he touched her hair. It was tangled, hanging rich about her shoulders. His fingers curled into it. "I want you."

She felt her knees tremble, and flames shot in all directions from somewhere in the pit of her stomach. She knew she had to ignore her sudden excitement. His admission meant nothing except that he was a normal male animal, and she was handy.

"I know," she said steadily. "And I want you. But I've decided I can't have you."

She stepped around him and walked across the yard. She didn't look back as she climbed the steps and entered the house.

The door closed and the porch light went out, leaving Joe alone in the night.

Chapter Six

The following week Andy threw herself into the job at the Fabian house. She had learned long ago that engrossing work was the best thing ever invented to help one forget trouble, and the Fabian job was just what she needed. The banker's wife had asked for Andy's help in planning the redecoration project. Andy's favorite jobs were those where she was allowed some creative input, and she riffled through her folders crammed with pictures clipped from home decorating magazines, looking for ideas.

In the master bedroom, for which Nelda Fabian had chosen a plain striped wallpaper, Andy suggested a companion paper with a bolder floral design for one wall and a wide floral border to tie it all together. Federal-blue vertical blinds for the window picked up the blue in the wallpaper.

With Andy's encouragement, Nelda added a few more daring touches to the other rooms and seemed enormously pleased with her own courage.

"You come up with ideas I'd never have thought of, Andy," Nelda told her. "You have a knack for picturing how a room will look when it's completed. You should be an interior decorator."

"I'm glad you like my suggestions, Nelda," Andy said, "but I enjoy working with my hands as well as with my head." Nevertheless she was inordinately pleased by the woman's compliments. It was nice to be told that she was capable and talented. All she seemed to be getting from other quarters these days was criticism.

On Tuesday, she became so engrossed in wallpapering the Fabians' master bedroom that she didn't think about Tony's ball game until she was driving home at five o'clock. The game had been scheduled for one o'clock that afternoon. She might have been able to make it for the last few innings at least, but she'd been so deep in her work that she'd forgotten all about it.

She was assailed by guilt. How could she have forgotten? She'd managed to go to Brad's game last week, something she was sure Tony would point out to her. Oh, dear, Tony would probably think she was playing favorites, when she had always bent over backward to be fair. She sighed with resignation as she pulled into the post office parking lot. It was too late to redeem herself in Tony's eyes today. She'd just have to make sure she was in the bleachers the next time his team played at home.

In the post office, she opened her box. Still no sup-port check from Harley, not that she'd really expected one. The box held only two utility bills. Next she opened Bo's box and took out a handful of mail, most of it either contest related or junk advertising. Ap-parently the people who ran some of the contests Bo entered sold their mailing lists to direct-mail advertis-ers.

Back in the van, Andy drove toward home. Had Joe been at Tony's ball game? she wondered. She hoped they hadn't both disappointed Tony. Was it possible she'd "forgotten" the game because she wanted to avoid making conversation with Joe for two or three hours? More than possible, she admitted with rueful honesty. Conversations with Joe were invariably un-settling, and his silences could be even more disturb-ing. Andy had learned that it wasn't quite safe to relax fully when he was around. Maybe unconsciously she had known that keeping up her guard with Joe was becoming a more difficult feat each time she saw him.

As she drove the last few blocks to her house, she framed her apology for Tony. It was a bit disconcert-ing to discover that she didn't need it immediately. Tony and Brad weren't around. Bo wasn't either.

The three of them didn't show up until dusk. Andy went out to the porch as they climbed out of the pickup. "Sorry we're late, Andy," Bo greeted her. "I hope you haven't been worried about us."

"No, not worried," Andy said. "What kept you?"

Tony clambered up the porch steps. "After my ball game, Grandpa had to practice for his commercial some more. Joe let Brad and me watch."

"Tony, I'm really sorry I didn't make it to your game," Andy said, bracing herself for accusations followed by pouting.

"Aw, that's okay, Mom," Tony said breezily. "Joe and Grandpa and Brad were there."

Stunned by his reaction, Andy could only laugh. She kissed the top of his tousled head. "Who won?"

"We did," said Tony proudly. "I played right field—and I caught two flies. Coach said I'd be ready for the big leagues if I kept that up."

Brad had come up on the porch and was standing behind Tony. He looked at his mother and rolled his eyes at Tony's blatant self-congratulations. Andy winked at him. "Gosh, I'm impressed."

"Joe likes the commercial inside the domino parlor better than outside," Brad informed her.

"So he's going to film it there," Bo added. He had walked across the yard and was resting one foot on the bottom porch step. "Maybe next week. You know, I'll be sorry to see the end of it. I'm having fun."

"I'm glad, Pop," Andy said.

"You should've seen Mr. Connelley," Brad said.

"Yeah, he had more fun than anybody," Tony added. "He laughed so much he almost choked. They kept having to start over because they're supposed to be having a serious domino game, but Mr. Connelley couldn't stop laughing."

"He told Joe to keep him in mind if he took a notion to turn anybody else into a TV star," Bo said, chuckling. "Said he might even consent to going against nature and wearing dentures in a case like that."

"Well," Andy observed, "sounds like everybody had a good time today. Pop, I made chicken salad. Want to come in and eat with us?"

"No, thanks, Andy. I'm pooped. I'm going to go stretch out on the couch." He grinned up at her. "I always thought actors had it easy, but I'm finding out that rehearsing can take the starch out of you."

As she followed Brad and Tony into the house, Andy discovered that she was grateful to Joe for calling a rehearsal after the ball game. For one thing, it had taken Tony's mind off her failure to appear. For another, practicing for the commercial was giving Bo a new stature with his friends.

She tried to ignore the worrisome thought that in recent days Joe seemed to be spending as much time with her family as she did. It wasn't that she minded him paying so much attention to Brad and Tony; it was just that she didn't want them to get too attached to someone who could be transferred back to Detroit at any time.

She shook off the vague worry as she set the boys' dinner on the kitchen table. Cold chicken salad, crunchy with celery and walnuts, was usually a favorite summer evening meal, but both boys merely picked at the food. They were obviously worn out from the day's activities. Finally, Brad confessed, "Joe bought us candy bars and pop at the domino parlor."

Andy pressed her lips together on a terse criticism and sent the boys to shower and get ready for bed. The phone rang while she was clearing the table. She grabbed the receiver from the wall at the end of the kitchen counter.

"How's everything, Andy?" a male voice boomed.

Harley. He sounded as nonchalant as though they'd talked last week instead of six months ago. " 'Everything' covers a lot of territory, Harley," Andy said.

He laughed. "Ain't it the truth. Well, how're you?"

"I'm okay. Are you still in Miami?"

"Tampa, but not for long. I'm moving to Gainesville next week. I'll let you know my new address when I get one. Listen, I'm sorry it's been so long since I touched base, but you know how it is."

She knew how it was, all right. He'd decided six months without a word was about the limit of her patience. Harley didn't want anybody thinking about going to court. "Afraid so, Harley."

There was a pause, and then a hesitant laugh. She could picture him leaning back in a chair, his big hands clasped behind his head, the phone clamped between shoulder and jaw, a dimple twinkling in his right cheek. Harley was a handsome man. It irked her that, at nineteen, she'd been so dazzled by his good looks she hadn't seen beyond them.

"Sugar, I know you're mad at me about the support checks...."

Sugar? God, the man still thought he could dazzle her with his charm. "It's been six months, Harley."

"Hell, has it been that long? Well, never mind. I'm going to catch up with what I owe you—"

"It's not me you owe, Harley," Andy corrected. "It's your sons."

"Yeah, well, that's what I mean. You'll get the money, as soon as I get it. Which won't be long now, I promise you. A friend of mine let me in on the sweetest deal you ever heard of. Four thou was all it took to buy into the business.''

Four thousand would have taken care of the child support for the past six months, Andy thought sourly.

"I can't believe I was so lucky," Harley enthused. "Solar water heaters, Andy. It's the wave of the future, and I'm getting in on the ground floor."

Andy tipped her head back and stared at the ceiling. It was all so familiar.

Minks, Andy. Do you know you can raise hundreds of the critters in a little bit of space? We'll be rich!

Mail order, Andy. That's the coming thing. People nowadays are too busy to go out to shop when they can buy in the comfort of their own home. For three thou, we can get into the business.

Everlasting light bulbs, Andy.

Designer look-alike watches, Andy.

Now it was solar water heaters.

"Wonderful."

"I knew you'd understand why I haven't been able to send the money if I just explained it to you. You always were a reasonable woman, Andy."

Good old Andy, she mused wearily. "By the way, Tony's birthday was the sixth."

"The sixth? Of this month? Hell, you're right. I forgot! Well, I'll pick up something tomorrow and send it to him. What's he want?"

"Don't bother. I bought him a backpack and put your name on it. He'll probably thank you for it when you talk to him."

"Say, that was real decent of you, Andy. Can't think how I ever let you slip through my fingers." He paused in case she wanted to pick up on the opening. When she didn't respond, he went on, "You know I miss you like hell, don't you? I still think we could work something out if you'd—"

"Harley, we're running up your phone bill," Andy said hastily, "and you still haven't talked to the boys. I'll call them."

"Andy, can't we just talk about it? Geez—"

"Bye, Harley." Andy left the phone to dangle on its cord and went into the hall. "Brad, Tony, your father's on the phone."

"Tony's in the shower," Brad said as he rushed past her, his pajama top flying open, and grabbed the receiver. "Hi, Dad!"

Andy opened the bathroom door and called, "Tony! Phone!" Then she went into her own bedroom and shut the door. She stretched out on her bed and leafed through a magazine, waiting for the boys and Harley to finish their conversation.

Even with the door closed, she could hear Brad bringing Harley up to date on his ball games and describing the three home runs he'd hit that summer. A few minutes later, she heard Tony telling Brad to hurry up and give him the phone. Then Andy gritted her teeth as she heard Tony enthusing over his backpack.

Finally Tony was saying, "Really, Dad? Honest? Oh, wow, that'd be great! Wait'll I tell Brad! Okay, Dad. You'll call us again real soon and let us know which weekend? Okay. Bye, Dad."

Andy opened her door as Tony came barreling down the hall, followed by Brad who was yelling, "What'd he say? What'd he say?"

"Mom, listen to this! Dad's gonna take me and Brad on a camping trip!"

"He is? When?"

"He said either the last weekend in June or the first weekend in July. Brad and I are supposed to figure out a good place to go around here."

"Whoopee!" Brad yelled.

"I'm gonna start putting stuff in my backpack right now," Tony said.

"Yeah, me, too. Let's go make a list of what we'll need, Tony."

Frowning in dismay, Andy watched them disappear into Brad's bedroom, talking excitedly, their heads together. She closed her door and dropped back down on her bed. No matter how many promises Harley broke, the boys continued to accept his feeble excuses and believe him the next time. Well, maybe they had to, she thought wearily. If they doubted their father's word, they'd probably have to deal with a lot of buried feelings that they weren't ready to look at yet.

Andy hadn't the faintest hope that the camping trip would ever materialize. And she was the one who would be there to witness a disappointed Brad and Tony when it finally came home to them that their father had broken yet another promise. Harley would soothe his own conscience by telling himself that good old Andy would handle it. If she could have put her hands on Harley at that moment, she could have cheerfully throttled him.

* * *

The trick to being a single mother, Andy had discovered, was to do the best she could with each day's problems as they arose and not try to solve future problems until she was faced with them. Ninety percent of what you worry about never happens, so Bo told her frequently. That might be generally true, but in the case of Harley, she knew him well enough to predict what he would do. Harley's enthusiasm was close to the surface, but he lost interest when the newness of an idea wore off or when hanging on to it caused him inconvenience. He was big on talk and short on follow-through.

Though she succeeded for hours at a time in not borrowing trouble, worry about the consequences of Harley's breaking another promise in the near future surfaced from time to time. Sometimes she thought it would be easier if Harley dropped out of their lives for good. But even as she had the thought, she told herself she was being selfish. It might be easier for her, but not for the boys. Any contact at all with their father was surely better than none.

She remained noncommittal as, during the next two days, the boys made elaborate plans for the camping trip with their father. They made lists. Lists of clothing they would need. Lists of food and menus for two days. Lists of cooking utensils and other equipment and supplies. Twice they rode their bikes the three miles to the city lake to search out good camp sites. Andy watched and listened and kept silent.

By the next week, she had bottled up a lot of frustration and resentment. It wasn't healthy, she knew, and served no purpose to be angry with Harley. Maybe this time, she told herself hopefully, he'll come through for Brad and Tony. Maybe, but she wouldn't bet on it.

When Bo came over Wednesday evening to ask if she and the boys wanted to go out for ice cream, she declined for herself, but willingly agreed to the boys' going.

"They filmed the commercial this afternoon," Bo told her.

"So I heard from the boys. Are you pleased with the way it turned out?"

"I think so, but I guess I won't know for sure till I see it on film. Joe promised to bring over a videotape as soon as he gets one. He's real optimistic about it. They're going to show it in test markets on the East and West Coasts first. So it could be months before we know if it'll go nationwide."

"If Joe's optimistic, I'd say that's a good sign," Andy said. "He seems to know his business."

"Yeah." Bo gave her a contemplative look, and she knew he wanted to ask how things stood between her and Joe. He was clearly still hoping that a relationship would develop, but he tactfully avoided asking about it. "Get in the truck, boys," he said. "Andy, we might go by the domino parlor after we have our ice cream. We'll be back in an hour or so."

Andy smiled. Bo had been spending even more time than usual at the domino parlor recently, basking in his new prominence with his cronies. "Fine, Pop." She waved to them from the porch as they drove off.

It was growing dark. Dressed in shorts and a halter, Andy sat down, stretched out her bare legs, leaned back on the porch steps and gazed up at the slate-colored sky. Dozens of stars were already visible, and a quarter moon hung over the oak tree at the corner of the yard. The night smelled of honeysuckle and new-mown grass. A cricket hummed in the clump of tiger lilies to the right of the steps.

The calm of the summer night caressed her. She took a deep breath and let it out slowly. How could she fret over her small problems amid such tranquillity? The vastness of the spangled sky certainly put things in a better perspective.

Joe turned his car onto Andy's street and braked in front of her house. He switched off the headlights and got out. He saw her sitting on the front steps. Her head and upper body were outlined in a rectangle of pale light from a living-room window. She had been avoiding him the past week, and for days he had vacillated between trying to break through her defenses and letting the situation ride. Finally, he'd decided on a compromise. He'd make contact, then wait to see how she reacted before thinking about the next step.

He'd become a loner these past two years. Work had become his companion, his mistress. For the most part, it was easier to avoid the emotions that accompanied personal relationships. But recently he'd been reminded that the emotions didn't disappear; they merely went into hiding temporarily.

He could see now that even his work would eventually be affected by his withdrawal from life. He'd get stale without intimate contact with other people. By touching his buried emotions, Andy and her family had made him realize that. He liked Bo, and he could easily fall in love with Andy's kids. As for Andy?

He was beginning to understand her. She was inherently generous and kind. She was sensitive and emotional, but he suspected she wasn't totally comfortable with all her feelings. Perhaps when her marriage failed, she'd decided, unconsciously, to concentrate on being a parent and deny her other needs.

But he wanted her. He didn't think it was merely because she was a challenge, but he'd spent two years repressing his physical needs, so he couldn't be sure. Whatever the reasons, he wanted her—which was why he was there, though he'd come prepared with an excuse. Because he knew that with Andy he'd have to be patient.

He flipped the stub of his cigarette away as he approached the house. "Nice night," he observed, stopping in front of her.

The light from the house didn't dispel the shadows in the hollows of his cheeks and around his eyes. He wore dress slacks and a short-sleeved dress shirt rumpled from the day's use. Evidently he hadn't been home since leaving the office. The top two buttons of his shirt were undone, and he'd left his jacket and tie in the car.

"If you came to see Pop, he's not at home," Andy said.

"I didn't come to see Bo," he murmured and drew a small package from his trousers pocket. "I brought these for Brad and Tony."

She took the parcel, which was wrapped in brown paper, and turned it over in her hand. "What is it?"

"Baseball cards. David, my son, had quite a collection. I thought your boys might like to have them."

"They'll love them." Brad, in fact, had recently started a collection, and naturally Tony wanted one, too. "Thank you." She set the package beside her on the step. "I'll give them to Brad and Tony as soon as they get home. They've gone to town with Pop."

"May I sit down?"

She nodded and drew her knees up to link her arms around them.

He sat beside her on the top step, leaning forward to rest his elbows on his knees. Looking straight ahead, into the night, he said, "You've been avoiding me."

"No..." She turned her head and studied his dark profile. She felt a tension in him that was belied by his casual posture. Unless she was projecting her own feelings onto him. "Why do you think that?"

Still he didn't look at her. "You haven't been to any more of Bo's rehearsals, and you weren't at Tony's ball game last week."

"I—I was working and forgot the game until it was too late. I'll make it up to Tony."

He turned his head. His eyes were only inches from hers, yet she couldn't read his expression in the darkness. "I assumed you didn't come because you knew I'd be there."

Unnerved by his closeness, she shifted a little away from him. "I really did forget. I've been preoccupied with my own problems this week."

He leaned toward her. "I'm a good listener if you feel like talking about it."

His arm brushed hers. It made her flesh tingle. She didn't move, and then she heard herself say, "We finally heard from Harley."

His hand slipped beneath her arm, and his fingers wound around her clasped hands. "Is he getting married again?"

She gave a nervous laugh and, unclasping her hands, entwined the fingers of her left hand with his. She leaned back. "No. I only wish he would. Maybe he'd stop..." She paused, suddenly self-conscious.

"Asking you to come back to him?"

"How did you know?"

He shrugged. "It figures. He'd be a fool not to want you and the boys back."

His words sent a little thrill through her blood, but she clamped down on it. "Sometimes I think Harley says he wants us back because he thinks it's expected of him. I don't really care why he does it. That isn't what's bugging me."

She fell broodingly silent, and he peered at her in the darkness. "If you don't love him, he shouldn't be able to bug you."

"Easy to say," she murmured. "And it would be true if Brad and Tony weren't in the middle. Now he has them all worked up over a camping trip. They've talked of little else for the past week. They've even found a campsite out near the city lake."

"You don't think Harley will show up to go camping with them?"

"I'm ninety-nine percent sure he won't. Harley isn't the outdoor type. He doesn't even like backyard cookouts. He likes air-conditioning and hot showers and clean sheets. He's never been camping in his life."

Joe was silent for a long moment, knowing what he wanted to say, but not sure if he should. Finally, he decided to be honest with her. "It's not your problem, Andy." He felt her draw away from him.

"Oh, yeah? What am I supposed to tell the boys when Harley doesn't show up?"

"How about the truth? If you try to soften the blow by making up excuses for Harley, you'll only succeed in adding to your own resentment. Simple honesty would make everything less complicated."

She didn't answer right away, but he felt her give him a piercing stare and knew he'd made her angry. Feeling her slipping away from him, he cupped her bare shoulder, rubbing his thumb over her collarbone. Motionless, she stared at him. He bent and touched his lips to hers, without pressure or force. A tremor ran through her, and he moved his lips over hers, daring her to resist her own needs.

Andy was determined to do just that. She struggled to control the fast drumming of her heart, and turned her head to break the kiss. "They're my kids," she managed in a hoarse whisper. "I'm the one who has to decide what's best for them."

"You don't have to keep reminding me of that." He caught her chin with one hand and turned her face back to him. He kissed her once, hard and quick. "I know whose kids they are." He reminded himself that he'd come there knowing that Andy would require patience. He released her and rose, fighting his own heated blood. "Tell Bo and the boys I'm sorry to have missed them."

Andy immediately regretted her unnecessary sharpness. She wanted to call him back, but he was gone.

Chapter Seven

Bo's voice on the telephone was buoyant with excitement. "Andy, can you and the boys come over?"

"Sure. What's up?"

"Joe's here and he has my commercial on videotape. He's connecting a VCR to my TV right now so we can watch it."

It was Friday, and Andy hadn't seen Joe since Tuesday night. Wednesday, while Andy was at work, the boys had phoned his office to thank him for the baseball cards. As Andy had expected, the cards were a big hit with Brad and Tony.

Thursday afternoon, Andy had been in the bleachers for Tony's ball game, but Joe wasn't there. Once she realized he wasn't coming, she discovered that she was unsure how she felt about his absence. Relieved, she didn't examine her reactions too closely because she didn't want to fully explore her feelings about Joe.

However, in a town the size of Neptune she couldn't avoid him altogether, and she didn't want Bo to think she wasn't eager to see the tape.

"We'll be right over, Pop."

She dashed to the bathroom to brush her hair and add a bit of color to her lips. There wasn't time to change from the well-worn cotton slacks and knit shirt she'd donned between her evening shower and dinner preparations. Nor was there any reason to, she told herself.

When Andy and the boys arrived, Bo had arranged five chairs in a semicircle before the TV set.

"All we need is popcorn," Andy observed.

Joe, in jeans and a cotton shirt, was leaning back in a chair, smoking a cigarette. He caught Andy's gaze and smiled slowly. Brad and Tony went to him immediately and began telling him about the new notebooks with plastic-covered pages they'd bought for displaying their baseball card collections.

Andy watched them, thinking that so many adults only pretended to listen to kids. But not Joe. He gave them his undivided attention, and the boys knew it. That was probably why they'd grown so fond of him in such a short time. Finally Brad and Tony, choosing to ignore the chairs Bo had so carefully arranged, flopped on the floor directly in front of the television set.

It would look odd, Andy reflected, if she left empty chairs between hers and Joe's. Making a swift decision, she sat beside him. "How're you?"

"Good. I think we've got a winner."

"For Pop's sake, I hope so."

"Come on, Grandpa," Brad called to Bo, who was moving about the room, fidgeting with lights. "Let's see your commercial."

"In a minute," Bo said, switching the floor lamp in the corner to low.

"He's really taking this seriously," Andy said as she watched Bo squint at the blank TV, then turn the floor lamp up a notch.

Joe nodded. "It could get to be serious business if the commercial strikes a lot of funny bones. No way of knowing till we test it, but a few stars from commercials have become so popular they're practically cult figures.

"Pop a cult figure?" Andy shook her head. "That would take some getting used to."

"I know you've had your doubts about this whole thing," Joe said.

"At first, I thought you were trying to make Pop look bad."

"I wouldn't do that."

"I believe you—now," she said slowly. "But I've also been worried that nothing would come of this in the end—you said yourself there's no way of predicting the outcome—and then Pop would be humiliated in front of his friends."

He grinned at that. "It would take a lot more than a scrapped commercial to humiliate Bo."

"I suppose you're right," Andy agreed. She knew what he was thinking—that Bo didn't need her worrying about his feelings. Now that she thought about it, Bo would resent any attempts she might make to shield him from disappointment. It annoyed her, though, that Joe kept forcing her to confront her tendency to rescue those she loved. "It's good to know you've gotten what you want."

His gaze was rueful, and it was a moment before he responded. "Are we still talking about the commercial?"

"We certainly are," she said dryly.

Casually he reached behind her to stub out his cigarette in an ashtray on the coffee table. Andy hadn't noticed the ashtray before; Bo must have bought it especially for Joe's visit. Joe's arm pressed against her shoulder and, for an instant, his chin brushed her hair. She gripped the edge of her chair as he withdrew his arm, and relaxed as he settled back in his seat again. "Do I make you nervous?" he asked quietly.

"Of course not."

"Then why won't you go out with me again?"

She lifted both brows. "I've been very busy."

Idly, he threw his arm across the back of her chair and cupped the back of her neck in his hand.

Andy glanced nervously at the boys, but their eyes were trained on the television set. "Joe—"

"I told Bo I wanted to see you alone this evening," he said softly. "He agreed to keep the boys here while we go out for a bit."

Ingratiating himself with her father was dirty pool, she thought. The gentle rubbing of his fingers on the back of her neck sent tremors of alarm through her, but the look she gave him was cool. "My father doesn't make dates for me, and I haven't agreed to anything."

"You will," he murmured as Bo finished adjusting the lighting to his satisfaction and turned on the television. The tensing of Joe's fingers on her neck revealed that he was frustrated.

"Sure of yourself, aren't you?"

"Far from it," he admitted under his breath. His fingers released her. His eyes were calm but determined as he grinned at her. "Let 'er roll, Bo," he said out loud, and Bo punched the on button of the VCR, then took the chair on the other side of Joe.

Sitting forward, Andy focused her attention on the screen. There was a long shot of Neptune's main street—the bank and department store on the right, the hardware store and bakery on the left. The camera zoomed in quickly on the domino parlor. Then they were inside with a close-up shot of Bo, Curtiss Rankin, Barney Morse, and Dermas Connelley around a table, dominoes laid out before them. As the camera panned, Curtiss leaned back and tugged at his suspenders. Barney chomped down on the cigar sticking out of the corner of his mouth, making it wobble. Dermas sent a toothless grin around the table as though he were fighting to keep from breaking into laughter.

With a flourish, Bo played a domino, pulled on the bill of his cap and looked into the camera. "I never lived anywhere but Neptune, Nebraska, in my whole life," he drawled, and the boys cracked up.

A grin tugged at the corners of Andy's mouth. "Shhh, guys. We can't hear."

On the television screen, Bo was saying, "I been down to the barn and back—in a manner of speakin'. When NM came out with these Neptune auto-mo-biles, I liked the name—" he touched his cap where white letters spelled out Neptune, Nebraska "—nat-urally—but I don't buy cars fer the name. I buy 'em for the quality and dependability." Bo slapped an-other domino down and chortled, "Looks like I win again, fellas." He rose and looked back at the cam-era. "I want a car that's a winner, too. That's why I bought me a new Neptune."

Tony rolled onto his back, laughing. "You're funny, Grandpa!" Andy had to agree. Bo and his cronies came across as exaggerations of themselves, but with such a brief span of time to work in, exaggeration was essential.

"Yeah," Brad agreed. He was sprawled on his stomach, chin in hand. "Let's watch it again. I wanta get a better look at Mr. Connelley."

Bo got up to rewind the tape.

"I'll leave the tape and VCR with you for a few days, Bo," Joe said.

"Good. I'll invite my pals over tomorrow night to see it." The whirling tape clicked to a stop. "You don't have to watch it again, Joe. You've probably seen it a dozen times already."

"More than that," Joe said. "What I'd like to do right now is take Andy out for a drink."

Andy shot him a piercing glare, which Joe ignored.

"Sure, you two go ahead," Bo said magnani-mously. "The boys and I will look at the tape again."

Joe got to his feet and extended his hand. "Come on, Andy," he said cheerfully, "we could both use some fresh air."

Andy realized that Bo, Brad and Tony were all looking at her expectantly. She felt trapped. Watching her, Joe saw the uncertainty in her eyes. For a moment, he stared at her, wishing he hadn't been so high-handed. "Andy, if you'd rather not . . ."

"No." She reached for his hand and let him pull her to her feet. "Let's go." Resigned, she walked across the room and opened the door without looking back.

The night was warm and still except for a cricket singing in the yard. She tossed her hair back from her face and strode briskly to Joe's car. She opened the passenger door and got in without having said another word.

We'll go for a drink, and then I'll ask him to bring me home, she told herself as Joe walked around the car to the driver's side. It did feel good to get out of the house for a bit. Joe slid in beside her. "You ticked off at the way I handled that?"

"Not really," she admitted. "I could have said no."

"Why didn't you?"

"I'm not quite sure."

He grinned and started the engine.

"You were right about the commercial," Andy said. "All my worries were unnecessary. It's good, isn't it?"

"In my opinion, it's very good."

"That's enough for me. You obviously know what you're doing."

"In my professional life, yes."

She looked over at him. In the light from the dash she saw his deprecating half smile. "Not in your personal life?"

"I haven't had a personal life for some time," he said simply.

The flat admission touched her. His interest in her family was probably the first he'd had in anything besides work since he lost his wife and children. Surely she could be generous enough not to begrudge him that. He just needs somebody to talk to, she reflected, reminding herself again that the only safe relationship she could have with Joe was friendship. Then she turned to look out the side window as they left the main street of Neptune behind. "I thought we were going somewhere for a drink."

"The drinks are in the cooler in the back seat. I thought we'd drive out to the lake."

Andy started to protest, but decided not to make an issue out of it. "And you said you weren't sure of yourself," she chided him.

"Let's say I was optimistic."

She chuckled and turned sideways in the seat. She reached in back and lifted the cooler lid. "What do we have?"

"Beer and soft drinks."

"What, no champagne?"

He chuckled. "I'm out of practice. What can I say?"

She pulled cans from the cooler until she found a strawberry soda and flipped the tab. "What're you having?"

"I'll wait till we stop." He had taken the lake road away from town, and was driving slowly along a narrow blacktop lane, its surface dappled by the full moon shining through the sheltering trees. On their right, the lake glistened like black glass.

They passed a couple of cars parked off the road overlooking the water. Did Joe know that the lake road was where teenage boys brought their girlfriends after dinner or a movie? She took a swallow of soda and decided not to mention it. Joe veered off the lane and rolled to a stop beside a big oak tree whose branches reached out over the water. He got a beer from the cooler and said, "Let's walk."

Andy welcomed the suggestion. Walking somehow seemed less intimate than staying with Joe in the parked car, in a setting where she remembered necking with high school boyfriends.

They strolled along the verge of the lake. "I always loved it out here," Andy said. "When I was in high school, I came here a lot with my friends—for picnics, hikes, swimming, and stuff like that."

"Making out?"

She smiled. "I was wondering if you realized that this is the local lovers' lane."

He linked his hand with hers. "I figured it had to be. It's the most romantic setting around here, and there's plenty of privacy."

"Well, I came here with a boyfriend a few times." She grew wistful. "Gosh, that seems like a long time ago."

He squeezed her hand. "You have happy memories of your childhood."

"Yeah," she agreed. "I guess that's why I wanted to bring Brad and Tony back here after Harley and I split. What about you? What was your childhood like?"

He tipped his beer to his mouth before he answered. "My parents were in their forties when I was born. My brother was seventeen, my sister sixteen, by that time. My folks thought they'd about raised their family, so they weren't exactly ecstatic about starting over." They neared a trash receptacle, and he tossed in his beer can. Andy drained her soda and dropped her can in, too.

"They'd always planned to retire early, travel around the country pulling a trailer, stopping whenever the notion struck them," Joe continued. "Then I came along, and they had to postpone retirement until I'd finished high school. They never said a thing to me about any of that, of course, but kids overhear conversations and sense a lot that they don't hear. They weren't demonstrative people in the first place, so we sort of went our separate ways. I left for college at eighteen and never went back, except for a few holidays."

Their steps had become slower and slower as Joe talked, and now they stopped completely. Andy peered up at him. It was easy to imagine him as a child, hungry for love and attention, but too proud to admit it to parents who hadn't wanted him. How different from her own upbringing. Her parents had let her know almost daily how much she was loved and wanted, and had cherished her all the more because they were unable to have other children.

"Oh, Joe, I'm sorry."

He shrugged carelessly. "They did the best they could. I stopped resenting them a long time ago. But I promised myself if I ever had a family, we'd talk about our feelings and spend time together." She sensed as much as saw the sudden pain in his expression, and she thought she knew what he was feeling. "Most of the time we managed that pretty well," he went on finally. "I didn't let my work consume me until—afterward."

Lifting her face, she kissed his cheek in a gesture of simple understanding. Taking his hand, she led him to a stone bench, one of many that were scattered around the lake. "Would you like to talk about them?" she asked softly.

He put his arm around her and let out a long breath. Understanding that he needed the comfort of simple human contact, she leaned her head lightly against his shoulder. From where they sat, she could see the big perfect circle of the moon's reflection in the far side of the lake.

"I did my share of carousing in college, but all I ever really wanted was a family of my own. I met Miriam when I was a senior. She was pretty and generous and good-natured, characteristics I didn't associate with my mother. Now I know that I was also attracted to the fact that Miriam had no real career aspirations. She was barely getting by in her college courses because she simply wasn't interested. She just wanted to get married and have children and stay at home with them. I think she was comfortable with me because I didn't want to change her. She used to say it was a good thing she found me because she'd been born too late for anybody else."

Andy listened to Joe with surprise. She couldn't think of him as old-fashioned. Unless you called being a family man old-fashioned, which Andy didn't. She saw it as a sign of strength and maturity. His revelations helped her understand why he had chosen to retreat into work since his wife's death. If he wanted another old-fashioned girl whose sole desire was to keep the home fires burning, there weren't many of them around. Andy herself enjoyed her work. It was something of her own that she didn't have to share with anyone. It gave a dimension to her life that she'd never had when she was married—an identity that had nothing to do with her being somebody's daughter or wife or mother—and she wouldn't want to give it up.

"Sometimes," Andy mused, "people..." She faltered as she realized that what she was thinking could be construed as a criticism of Joe's wife.

He tilted her chin and studied her face. "People what?"

She gave a little shake of her head. "Nothing. I was thinking aloud."

"I want to know what you're thinking—all of it."

She hesitated, then said, "All right. Sometimes people make choices because the choices represent security, and they're afraid of risks." His expression thoughtful, he gently brushed her hair away from her face. "It's merely a general observation," she added. "I'm not suggesting it applied to Miriam—or to you."

"I know," he murmured, "and if you live long enough, you learn that nothing is really secure. Anything can be gone in an instant of time."

Like Miriam and his children. "I've often thought that growing up is discovering how to live delicately balanced in the present moment, learning from the past without getting mired in regrets and planning for the future without forgetting to live today." Impulsively, she lifted his hand to press a soft kiss in the palm. "End of lecture."

The gesture disconcerted him. Dropping his arm from her shoulders, he cupped her face in his hands. She seemed to him very vulnerable, yet she had a strength that was surprising. Perhaps she'd gotten it from her parents, or maybe from having to be the solid one in her marriage. "You're a smart lady, Andy."

She smiled. "Does that surprise you?"

"No, but in spite of what you say, you don't seem willing to take many risks yourself."

She laughed softly. "Maybe I got that out of my system when I was married to Harley."

"If the Wright brothers had felt that way after the first try, we might not have jet planes today."

"Maybe." She stood abruptly. "I think we'd better head back to town now."

He got to his feet and kept her from walking away from him by placing both hands on her shoulders. She looked up at him guardedly. She appeared very beautiful to him. It was a natural beauty that would only have been diminished by artifice or pretense. He wanted her, and for the first time he realized that he also felt a strong need to give her joy. With a sudden tenderness, he brushed his lips over hers. "Was your marriage so bad that you've decided not to risk another relationship, ever?"

"No, but it made me cautious." Any risks she took now would be calculated ones. An affair with Joe would be like betting her life savings on one throw of the dice in Vegas. She knew that he wanted her—he was lonely. And she knew that Joe wasn't the type for a casual roll in the hay with somebody he barely knew. But his deepest emotions were still tangled up in the past. He'd talked to her about Miriam, but Andy had the odd feeling that he had left far more important things unsaid. Perhaps that was just as well, because she wasn't sure she was strong enough to hear the rest. Joe was like no man she'd ever known before, and she had to proceed with care. Never had she been so physically drawn to a man, but that wasn't what frightened her. A mere sexual attraction could be satisfied. Instinctively she knew that if she wasn't very careful, she could fall deeply, desperately in love with Joe.

He watched the play of expressions over her face, unable to decipher them. Tenderly he traced the outline of her lips with one finger. "What are you thinking now?"

To tell him this time would be too dangerous. Instead she kissed him softly, quickly, and pulled away. "A woman likes to have a few secrets."

His eyes became very intense. "What would it take to get you to trust me enough so you'll risk letting me get close?"

She didn't reply right away, knowing that the question was involved and deserved an honest answer. At length, she said, "I don't know."

Joe accepted the answer as the best she could give him at the moment. They returned to the car. On the drive home, she sipped at another soda, seemingly lost in thought. Joe smoked a cigarette, content for the moment to have had a few private minutes with her.

At her door, he said, "I haven't given up, Andy."

She sighed. "I probably wouldn't like you nearly as well if you were the sort to give up easily."

He would have kissed her then, but she slipped from his embrace with the fluid grace of a deer.

Chapter Eight

Each evening for the next three, several townspeople arrived at Bo's house to view the tape. Bo served them cold drinks and cookies, and there were always two or three men who stayed to play dominoes. At which point, Andy suspected, Bo brought out the beer. Andy heard their muffled laughter until late at night. Bo was getting so much fun out of showing the commercial, Andy thought, that it was worthwhile, even if it didn't get good reviews in the test markets.

Monday, after the boys had gone to bed, she stepped out on the porch in her scuffs and cotton nightshirt. Too wide awake to retire for the night, she sat in the porch swing and kept it moving slowly by pushing with one foot. A cluster of fireflies winked in the yard, and a gentle breeze, pleasantly cool on Andy's bare arms and legs, stirred leaves in the surrounding trees. In the air there was the pungent hickory smell of food cooking on an outdoor grill.

Bo's windows glowed with light, and occasionally the sound of male voices reached Andy, though she couldn't make out what they were saying. Just as well, she thought with a smile. Bo and his cronies loved to tell each other raunchy tales—the raunchier the better.

Who was Bo entertaining tonight? she wondered. She turned in the swing to peer at the dark shadows of cars in Bo's drive and at the curb. One seemed to have the shape of Curtiss Rankin's '63 Mercury, which he'd bought new and pampered like a favorite child. Bo swore it had less than fifty thousand miles on it.

Andy couldn't identify the second vehicle in the drive, and she slid her gaze to the curb where two other cars were parked. With a little jolt of recognition, she realized that one of them was Joe's.

She hadn't seen or heard from him since their drive to the lake Friday night. Apparently he'd been at Bo's all evening. After what he'd said Friday night when he'd brought her home, she had expected to hear from him during the weekend. But he hadn't called, and today, driving to work and coming home, she had found herself hoping for a sight of him in his car or walking along Main Street.

Now, he was next door. He could easily have stopped off at her house before going to Bo's, but he hadn't. Had he changed his mind? Perhaps he'd decided that he wouldn't continue pressing her to see him, after all.

Her feelings about Joe were so mixed up that she could see the wisdom in that while at the same time being hurt by it. Andy, she reflected, you're nuts. One brick short of a load, as Bo would say. Crackers, as Brad and Tony would put it. All of the above.

She drew her legs up in the swing and rested her cheek on her knees. She'd told Joe in every conceivable way that she wanted him to back off. So why should she feel hurt when he obliged her?

Of course, she knew why. When it came to Joe Underwood, she was a mass of contradictions. On the one hand, she was incredibly attracted to him; on the other, she was scared spitless by that attraction. The chemistry between them was so strong that, when they were together, it set every nerve in her body quivering for his touch, while at the same time it created a panicked urge to run the other way. She sat in the swing, filled with dismaying reflections, until her eyelids grew heavy.

She heard raucous laughter from next door as she left the swing. She went to bed and fell asleep, hugging her pillow.

Wednesday evening, Brad and Tony met her with the news that they'd seen Joe at midday, coming out of a restaurant in town. He had loaded them into his car, and they had driven to the park and played catch for half an hour before he went back to work.

"Did you know he used to be a hotshot diver in college?" Brad asked Andy.

"No," Andy said. "Joe never mentioned that to me."

"He almost trained for the Olympics," Tony informed her.

"But he decided to get married instead," Brad said with a grimace of bemusement. He hadn't yet reached the age where girls were anything but a nuisance, and he couldn't fathom giving up a beloved sport to marry one.

"Yeah, and he used to go skiing all the time with his wife and his kids," Tony revealed. "Did you know his family got killed in a plane crash, Mom?"

"Mmmm. How did Joe come to tell you about that?"

"Tony asked him a lot of nosy questions, that's how," Brad said. "You could tell Joe didn't want to talk about it, either. It was really embarrassing."

"Well, *he* said he went skiing with his family," Tony protested. "I just wanted to know what happened to them."

"I hope you don't ask him any more personal questions," Brad said, "or he won't want to play catch with us anymore."

"Cool your jets, Bradley," Tony said, more from habit than temper. "Mom, can we go skiing sometime?"

"I don't know," Andy said. "I'd have to check into the cost."

"We could save our allowances," Brad said hopefully. "I'll save all the money I make mowing lawns, too. Maybe we'll have enough by next winter."

"Can we ask Joe to go with us?"

"Absolutely not, Tony!" Andy said. "Besides, we don't even know that we're going."

Tony heaved a sigh of disgust, then took another stab at pinning her down. "*If* we get to go?"

Andy decided that procrastination was the easiest way out. By next winter, Joe could've been transferred back to Detroit. Or he could have found other people to spend time with besides Andy's family. In either case, the question would be moot. "We'll talk about it then."

Tony flopped down on the couch and uttered the child's perennial summertime complaint. "There's nothing to do around here." He eyed the scuffed toe of his canvas shoe for a moment, then brightened. "At least Dad's taking us camping next weekend."

It had been days since either of the boys had mentioned the camping trip. Andy had been hoping against hope that they'd forgotten Harley's promise. She should have known better. "He hasn't called again," she ventured.

"He'll probably call before Friday," Brad said, looking at Andy as though for confirmation.

She said nothing.

"Anyway," Tony said belligerently, "next weekend's the first weekend in July. Dad didn't come last weekend, so he has to come next weekend. He said he would!"

Perfect logic. The fallacy was that with Harley there was a vast chasm between the word and the deed. "Sometimes things . . . come up," she said.

Tony glared at her. "Nothing will come up!" he stated and stomped out of the room.

After a moment, Brad asked, "Do you think Dad will come, Mom?"

"I hope so, honey."

Andy left it at that. She didn't know how to get hold of Harley, or she would have called and tried to shame him into coming. Instead, she avoided any further mention of the weekend. As the days passed, Tony became more and more cross and belligerent. Somewhere in the back of his mind, he suspects Harley won't be here, Andy thought. Her maternal instinct was to try to comfort Tony, but she knew he would resent it. As for Brad, he merely became quieter and more withdrawn. He spent the evenings in his room, reading and working on a ship model.

Late Friday night they'd still had no word from Harley. Tony said with at least surface confidence, "He'll probably be here early in the morning."

Tony was up at dawn, already short-tempered. All morning he took his foul mood out on Brad and Andy every time they crossed his path. Finally, Andy got angry. She grabbed Tony and gave him a good shake. "Young man, if you can't be civil to your brother and me, you can spend the rest of the day in your room!"

Tony burst into tears, ran to his room and slammed the door. Within minutes, Andy regretted her outburst, but she left Tony alone to calm down. Brad took the disappointment stoically, but he'd had two years more than Tony to see his father realistically. Andy was relieved that, by noon Saturday, Brad seemed to have shaken off his depression; he left the house to go biking with a friend.

By Sunday morning, Tony had apparently conquered his anger and was merely subdued as Andy drove to church. She'd packed a picnic lunch, and after the service they went to the park and spread their meal on a picnic table in the shade of a cottonwood tree.

When they'd eaten, the boys ran off to play Frisbee. They seemed to be in better spirits. Andy reflected that they'd come through another crisis created by Harley. How many more would there be before they stopped believing anything their father said?

After packing up the leftovers, Andy spread a quilt on the grass, slipped off her sandals and settled down with her back against the trunk of the cottonwood to read a mystery novel. After a few pages, she lifted her eyes and saw Joe walking across the grass toward her. He looked tanned and so handsome, in a white knit shirt and gray cotton trousers, that Andy's breath caught in her throat.

Marking her place in the book, she watched him steadily as he approached, her heart lifting. As casually as if they'd come to the park together, and he'd been away from her for only a few minutes, he dropped down on the quilt beside her. He laid a hand on her arm. "How are you, Andy?"

"Fine." She smiled, letting him know she didn't care that she hadn't heard from him for over a week. "You're looking relaxed and in fine fettle."

He grinned. "That sounds almost like you're glad to see me."

"Don't jump to any bizarre conclusions."

"Right," he said dryly. His gaze raked her. "You look pretty in that gold color." Andy had on a gold cotton blouse and a dirndl skirt splashed with huge gold and lime-green flowers. "It matches the freckles on your nose."

She tucked her knees up beneath her skirt and wiggled her bare toes. "Gee, you sure know how to make a person feel good, Underwood."

"I've been told I'm a dashing rogue," he responded with a twinkle in his gray eyes.

"By a senile great-aunt?"

He laughed and, stretching out, leaned back on his elbows. "Where are the boys?"

"Around here somewhere. I'm surprised you didn't see them as you crossed the park."

He ran his fingers over the back of her hand which lay on the quilt between them, then turned it over. "I only had eyes for you."

"Really?" she said lightly, stirred by the touch of his fingers tracing small circles on the inside of her wrist. "That's a little hard to swallow since I haven't seen you in ten days."

"I was at Bo's house one night last week."

"Were you?"

"I went by to get the tape and stayed to play dominoes with Bo and a couple of his friends. I kept hoping you'd come over." She started to draw her hand away, but he captured it.

"The distance from Pop's house to mine is the same as from mine to his."

"I thought about it," he admitted, "but I decided to stay away from you long enough to give you a chance to miss me."

Her eyes darted away from his and searched for the boys.

"Did you?" he persisted. He was getting impatient with the studied casualness.

She brought her eyes back to his. She was becoming weary of dishonesty. "Maybe. A little."

"Hallelujah. We're making progress."

"Are we?" Her blue eyes were very solemn.

He would have lifted her hand to his lips, but she drew it away. "I want to see you tonight—alone."

She rested her chin on her knees and tucked the hem of her skirt over her bare toes. Lord, she had missed him, and more than a little. What was there to fear? Nothing had happened the last time they were alone together, except that they'd gotten to know each other better. And she deserved a night out, didn't she?

"Well...this has been a particularly trying weekend. It would be nice to get away," she admitted.

"Bring your swimsuit," he said with a slow smile. "I'll bring dinner."

They were going to the lake. There was no other place to swim around Neptune.

She grinned suddenly. "I'll show you where I used to swim when I was a kid."

"Seven o'clock?"

"I'll have to see if Pop can keep the boys." Before she could say anything else, a Frisbee whizzed past with Brad and Tony in hot pursuit. Seeing Joe, they abandoned the chase and tumbled onto the quilt.

"Play Frisbee with us, Joe!" Tony begged.

Joe's eyes were warm on Andy. "Want to join us?"

She lifted her hair from the back of her neck with one hand. "No, thank you. Don't want to muss my clothes." She reached for her book. "I'll stay here and read."

Brad and Tony were already pulling Joe to his feet. He looked back over his shoulder as they dragged him away. "Seven," he mouthed silently.

Bo took Brad and Tony to a movie, saying it was simpler all around if they spent the night at his house. They drove off at six-thirty. The boys had balked at first, saying they'd rather go swimming with their mother and Joe, but eventually they'd been persuaded.

Andy sat in the porch swing and waited for Joe. Dropping a canvas bag containing a brush and towels beside her, she settled down and stretched her arms along the back of the swing. She gazed down the street, deserted at dinnertime, and tried to ignore the hungry rumbling of her stomach.

The sun was a globe of fire, sinking between two houses across the street. The whole of the western sky blazed with light and color, as though the day were having one last extravagant riot before being overtaken by night.

Andy watched the sky and the quiet street with mixed feelings. It had been a day of varied emotions. Harley's failure even to communicate with his sons over the past week, and their attempt to deal with another letdown had left her wrung out and edgy. The afternoon in the park seemed to have given the boys back their usual optimism and energy, and as a result she'd been able to relax.

Maybe her unguarded state of mind that afternoon accounted for her acceptance of Joe's invitation for tonight. *You are sending that man so many mixed messages, Andy,* she mused, *that he must wonder if you're completely sane.* Well, she wasn't going to worry about it, she decided, throwing back her head to let her hair sway with the gentle movement of the swing. She'd spouted all that wonderful-sounding stuff to Joe about living in the present, so tonight he'd follow her own advice, relax and go with the flow. She'd be uptight and responsible tomorrow.

The problem was, she thought as she stretched languidly, that over the past few years she'd lost sight of the fact that fun and relaxation were as important in life as work and duty. Enjoying the languid feeling that was creeping over her, she slid down until her head rested against the back of the swing. She closed her eyes and kept the swing rocking with her toes.

She was falling asleep and never wanted to move again when she felt a feathery weight resting on the top of her head. She stirred, yawned and reluctantly opened her eyes. The weight moved as two hands clasped her head lightly and warm lips brushed her forehead. Andy sighed with pleasure and tilted her head up.

Joe was standing behind her, head bent, smiling.

"Hi." She rose quickly and reached for the canvas bag.

"You looked so comfortable, I almost hated to wake you," he murmured. "You look beautiful and vulnerable when you're asleep."

She laughed and swung the bag by its drawstring. "It's the poor light. I hope you brought plenty to eat. It's been a long time since lunch."

"I don't think you'll have cause for complaint." He walked around from behind the swing and smiled down at her. "Is your bathing suit in that bag?"

"No, I'm wearing it under my clothes. There's no place to change out at the lake."

His gaze raked her cotton knit slacks and pullover top. "Shucks, I've been thinking that skinny-dipping would be fun."

"No way." Andy held out her hand. "Come on before I start eating the tiger lilies."

Joe drove to the far side of the lake where the grassy bank sloped gently down to the water. He opened the trunk and handed her a knitted cotton throw and a Styrofoam cooler. She walked halfway down the slope, spread the throw on the grass and called, "Shall I come and get another load?"

"I've got everything." He walked down to her and set some sacks and another cooler on the grass. He knelt and began to unpack.

"What can I do?" Andy asked.

"Nothing. This is my show. You sit and let me wait on you."

"Wonderful." She sat down, stretched her legs out and, leaning back, braced herself with her hands behind her. "I adore being pampered."

He was setting plates and silverware out on the comforter. "All beautiful women should be pampered occasionally."

"Oh?" She looked at him and saw that his angular, manly features were softened by the dusk. "How many beautiful women have you pampered in your checkered career?"

"Let's see, I think it was two hundred and eighty-five at last count."

She laughed, shaking back her hair. "Then you must be very good at it. I think I'm going to love this."

He gave her a lazy, thoughtful look. "I will, too." He lifted a bottle from one of the coolers, set two glasses on the closed lid and poured. "To a perfect evening."

Her fingers closed around the stem of the glass he handed her, and she clinked it against his before drinking. Fizz tickled her nose and cold, bubbly wine ran over her tongue. "Champagne," she murmured, savoring. "Delicious." Closing her eyes, she sipped slowly. "Ah, pure nectar. I can't believe you found champagne of this quality in Neptune."

He picked up a bowl and handed it to her, then sat down beside her. "I didn't. I've been saving this bottle a long time for a special occasion."

"I'm flattered." The boat-shaped bowl was cold, and she had to bring it nearer her eyes to be sure of its contents. Carrot and celery sticks, radish roses, tiny whole tomatoes and pickle spears nestled in a bed of crushed ice. "Oh, lovely!" She set the dish between them and munched on a crisp carrot sliver.

They crunched and drank in easy silence as the sky darkened from pewter to charcoal. Sheltered between two curving banks as they were, they felt no hint of a breeze. When Andy tipped back her head she could see twinkling stars. Below them the lake was glistening and still. The hushed silence was broken only by the far-off hooting of an owl.

Joe leaned back on an elbow, facing Andy. "Are you glad you came?"

"Oh, yes." Smiling, she looked at him, loving the way the pale moonlight touched his face with silver. "Of course, Brad and Tony may never speak to me again. When they heard we were going swimming, they put up quite a fuss. Pop mollified them by taking them to a Clint Eastwood movie."

"They've had a rough weekend."

"What? Oh, they told you about the camping trip."

"Brad did, while we were playing Frisbee." He reached for the champagne bottle and refilled their glasses. "I don't know how Harley lives with himself."

Andy lifted her shoulders in a shrug. "Very well, actually." She popped a radish rose into her mouth and drank more champagne. "It's easy to live with yourself when you're the center of your world." She sipped again. "Heavens, that sounds bitter, and I don't want to be bitter." She laughed ruefully. "It's just that I have to deal with Harley because of the boys, and I resent it sometimes."

He sat up and put his arm around her, pulling her close enough for her head to rest on his shoulder. "Let's forget Harley tonight. Drink some more champagne."

"Good idea." She brought her glass to her lips, then nestled her head more comfortably in the crook made by his neck and shoulder and sighed contentedly. "It's so peaceful here.'' He pressed his mouth against her temple and she tilted her face up to brush his lips with hers.

She wore no scent. She smelled of soap and clean hair and healthy skin, a natural smell that was specially Andy's. "I've had this spot picked out for a week, hoping you'd agree to come tonight." He kissed her again, but lightly, demanding nothing.

"What a calculating devil you are." When he chuckled, she felt his chest rumble where her arm touched it. "When I was a teenager, one of the favorite things to do was to sneak out here at night and go swimming. We'd all been forbidden to swim after dark because our parents thought it was too dangerous." She giggled suddenly. "So, of course, we all had to do it at least once every summer after we were fourteen or so. It was the local rite of passage, I suppose."

"You navigated the passage very well. You're a hell of a woman, Andy." His tone had turned grave.

She sat up and peered at his handsome face for a long moment. "Well, this woman is still hungry. What's the next course?"

He leaned forward and planted a kiss on her nose. "Your wish is my command, sweet lady." He got to his feet, and she heard the rustle of paper and aluminum foil. Then he was arranging food on two plates. With a flourish, he flipped out a cloth napkin and spread it over her knees. Then he handed her a plate and a fork.

"Smells scrumptious. What is it?"

"Fresh trout fillets sautéed in lemon butter with a sprinkle of dill. Asparagus spears with cream sauce, and wild rice."

Andy tasted the fish. It was still warm and mouth-meltingly tender. "Oh, I love it. Did you cook this yourself?"

"Of course."

"How clever of you!"

"I don't like to sound immodest, but I'm a man of many talents. Stick with me, and I'll introduce you to more of them."

The invitation in his words made her flesh tingle. She laughed and took a bite of perfectly seasoned rice. "I'm impressed. You can cook, and Brad tells me you're a hotshot diver, too."

"Too bad there's no diving board out here, or I could demonstrate. I could be talked into a race, though."

Andy wiped butter off her chin with her napkin. "You think you can beat me, huh?"

"I'm relatively confident, yes." She could hear the grin and the challenge in his voice."

"Lord, men can be so smug," she said without rancor.

He chuckled. "Woman can be so unrealistic."

"I'm a darned good swimmer," she observed.

"We'll see."

She let it go, and they talked desultorily until they'd finished eating. Then Andy stood and stripped off her outer clothing. She wore a brown tank suit that was made for swimming, not for looking pretty on the beach. Putting her hands on her hips, she looked down at him, waiting.

Joe unfolded his long length and came to his feet slowly, staring at her. The moonlight gilded her slender body and the hair tumbling down her back. She was the most exquisite thing he'd ever seen. "You're not afraid of getting a cramp, so soon after eating?"

"An old wives' tale," she scoffed. "Not scared I'll beat you, are you?"

He shook his head to clear his mind of the dreamy gauze that seemed to have descended on it, and stripped down to swimming trunks. "I was prepared to take it easy on you, but after that remark I show no mercy."

Andy squealed with sheer, rippling delight and streaked for the water. She dove in and then came up, splashing.

Joe followed her. The cool water calmed his heated skin, and he grunted with pleasure, pushed off with his feet and glided toward Andy. She swiped her dripping hair back and grinned at him.

"See that dark place over there, where that little finger of land comes out into the water? We touch that and return to this spot. Last one back's a rotten egg." She kicked off and heard him coming after her. She made hard, smooth strokes, swimming as fast as she could. By the time she reached the turnaround point, Joe was even with her and not even breathing hard.

She, on the other hand was panting. She hadn't swum since last summer. But she wouldn't give up. They started back, stroking side by side, and then Joe moved ahead easily and beat her to the starting place by several yards. He waited there, treading water. She found the lake bottom with her toes and shook back her hair. Then she relaxed and let the water buoy her up. She was breathing hard. "I'm out of practice."

He threw back his head and laughed. "Excuses, excuses." He drifted nearer. Beneath the water, his hands found her waist and drew her close.

With an indrawn breath, Andy discovered that she was caught in his arms. Her heart had begun to slow down, but now it speeded up again. The thud was like a muffled hammering in her ears.

"Winner claims the prize," he murmured and took her mouth with care and tenderness.

Andy's lips parted, and she made a little mewing sound of pleasure. His mouth was warm and wet and softly seeking. It was a sublime moment, crystallized in time like a perfect jewel.

Andy set herself to savoring it.

Chapter Nine

Joe let his hands flow over the water-slick skin of her back. Her flesh was as sleek as satin, and whispered beneath his fingers. She relaxed against him—as soft and as sweet as he'd imagined she would be. He cupped her hips in his hands to support her. Her lips were wet and cool, but they warmed quickly as he tasted them with infinite care. He was determined to pace himself to her rhythm, to explore totally, to savor.

Patience, he reminded himself, patience.

After long moments, her tongue sought his. Slowly he took the kiss deeper, luxuriating in each nuance of taste and touch, while he held her tightly against him. The need to crush her mouth with his, to grind his body against hers became harder to resist. The sliding of her thighs against his beneath the water was in-

credibly arousing, but he fought the hot urge to out-
pace her.

Andy relaxed her weight into his hands, letting him
hold her with her toes touching the sandy lake bottom. She felt as though she was being slowly drawn
toward the deep center of the lake, but she made no
effort to hold back. For just a little while, she wanted
to be free of the structure and restraints by which she
lived. The feeling of letting go was arousing. There
was no past to regret, no future to anticipate. There
was only this one superlative moment, when she would
allow herself to drift toward the dark whirlpool of
passion.

She loved the taste of his mouth. She feasted on it,
relished it, as she had relished the champagne they had
drunk. But soon his mouth was not enough; she
wanted to taste more of him. She cupped her hands on
either side of his face and let her mouth roam over his
chin, the prominent cheekbones, the bridge of his
nose, the wide brow. His moist skin, tasting faintly of
salt and lake water, heated as her lips touched it, and
her lips grew hot, as though she had contracted a fever from the contact.

Her warm, moist mouth brushed slowly over a wet
eyebrow, her sweet breath warming his skin. Joe en-
dured the slow, erotic exploration of his face until the
frustration was more than he could bear. With a
groan, he let her body slide lower against his while he
anchored her head with both his hands. His mouth
searched the contours of her face as hers had searched
his. He tasted the hollows of her eyes and the closed
lids. He nuzzled an earlobe and feathered her jawline

with frantic kisses. His tongue hungrily explored the corner of her mouth, and her lips trembled and sought his with blind need.

The low, patient call of an owl to its mate and the softly lapping water around them seemed to roll through Andy's blood. She wound her arms around Joe's neck and pressed the aching tips of her breasts against his chest. He sucked in his breath and hauled her hard against him. He trailed kisses up her throat, and then his mouth found hers again. His lips crushed hers, and she felt a shudder run through his body. The fingers sliding over her wet skin were no longer languid, but feverish. His arousal was hard against her stomach, and Andy's long pent-up passion erupted.

She whimpered and moved against him. With a low, guttural growl he fumbled with the straps of her bathing suit, pulling them down her arms. Gripping her waist, he lifted her and buried his face between her breasts.

"Andy...ah, Andy..."

His tongue traced one ripe curve to its center. His seeking mouth found a clenched nipple and drew it in. The hot, wet suckling of his lips and the stroking of his tongue sent uncontrollable spasms of pleasure streaking through her. Her hands ran over him, feeling the hard contours of his back and shoulders and arms. Going wild with what his mouth was doing to her, she drove her fingers through his wet hair and clutched convulsively. The pleasure was too exquisite to be borne. She could die of it, she thought dizzily.

With sudden desperation, she pulled his head back up. His mouth devoured her, tasting her lips, her tongue, and then impatiently racing over her face. His hands covered her breasts, and his palms pressed the hard, wet tips.

She moaned, "I didn't think...I didn't know." The words were a throaty whisper. Andy didn't recognize her own voice and she didn't even understand the meaning of what she'd said. She was stunned and completely out of control.

A desperate sound of need was wrenched from Joe. He pushed her straps lower, anchoring her arms at her sides. He lifted her breasts in his hands, suckling one and then the other, back and forth in a frenzy of passion. It felt as though his mouth were drawing out her very soul. Her head lolled back, and she moved her lower arms enough to clutch the sides of his lean hips with her fingers. She stood still as shudder after shudder shook her body.

Her flesh was hot, the lapping water soothing. She felt her body melting, as though she were becoming a part of the liquid all around them. Mingling, flowing, floating closer and closer to the dark, whirling eddy of mindlessness and overwhelming need. The sound of their breathing was loud in the quiet night. The darkness enveloped them in secrecy.

She swayed and closed her eyes. She wanted him with a desperation she hadn't known existed, wanted him inside her, wanted to wrap her body around him and lose herself. She tried to cry out to him to take her, but her mind was already too fuzzy to form the words. Her legs had no strength now, and only the water and her hold on Joe kept her upright.

He lifted his head. In the moonlight, her lovely face looked ethereal. Her heavy lids fluttered open, and she stared at him with glazed eyes. "Let's get out of the water," he managed. With shaking fingers, he pulled her straps back up to her shoulders. He swept her up and carried her to the bank.

She wrapped her arms around him and let her head fall to his shoulder. In the moonlight, the throw they had spread on the ground was lighter than the surrounding grass. She raised her eyes and saw the inky bulk of the car at the top of the bank and unbroken dark masses where tree branches were blocking out the starry sky. A faint gust of wind whispered in the leaves for a moment and then was gone.

Her gaze drifted back to the throw spread on the grass. A few minutes ago they had lounged there, relaxed, eating and drinking champagne, and she had felt calm and in control. Then they had gone into the water as though into another dimension, and everything had changed. Senses had been heightened to an almost painful sharpness. Buried hungers had rushed to the surface. The very air was charged with the magic that had been unleashed in the water.

Now the summer silence seemed to be listening, as though the night held its breath, waiting for the magic to be given full rein. Yet, as Joe laid her down on the spread, she felt the magic receding, and reason crowded in to take its place. She hadn't come there with any intention of letting things go so far. She had wanted this night with Joe, to hear his voice, to share his thoughts. She had never meant it to go beyond that, but she had deluded herself about the strength of her control.

They were two people who had been celibate too long and who found each other incredibly attractive physically. An explosive combination, but it was no more than that, Andy told herself. There were many reasons why she couldn't let it be more than that. Joe could be transferred back to Detroit any time, but even that obstacle could be overcome if Joe's dead wife weren't between them. She had to keep reminding herself of Miriam.

She lay very still as he bent over her. The liquid weakness still flowed through her body, but with less force than before because logic was dissipating it. The only sound in the night was their breathing, which was slower than it had been. Joe's head was surrounded by stars.

He kissed her softly, then lifted his head to stare down at her. "What's wrong, Andy?"

As he'd carried her up the bank, she'd grown perfectly quiet in his arms, and he'd sensed her withdrawal. Now, she looked up at him, her face a blank and her eyes dark and steady. Seconds ago, every nuance of her emotions had been clear to him, but suddenly he had no idea what she was feeling.

"I don't think I'm ready for this," she said quietly.

Her stillness was somehow unnerving, but he didn't want to believe her. He kissed her eyes closed. "You were, a few minutes ago."

Her eyes fluttered open; it was her only outward response. When he lifted his head, she was looking at him in that same intent and watchful way. "Yes," she said simply. "I wanted you. If I'm to be honest, I still do. But now I can think more clearly. It would be a mistake, Joe. You're no more ready for it than I am."

She thought of Miriam. He had given up a chance for a spot on the Olympic diving team to marry her. She thought of his instant rapport with her boys and of the gaping hole left in his life by the loss of his own children. She couldn't even be sure he would have looked at her twice if she hadn't come with a ready-made family. They had known each other such a short time, and there were too many unanswered questions between them. They hadn't even reached the point where they could ask each other those questions.

Words of denial rose in Joe's throat, but he wouldn't let them out. For the past two years, he'd denied his physical needs. That had been possible because a piece of him had been dead. But this woman with her freckled nose and her long legs had reached down inside him and resurrected that missing part. He couldn't even remember if Miriam had ever excited such a tumult of passion in him as Andy did. He wanted her so much that he ached with it. But he wouldn't argue and he wouldn't beg.

He levered himself to his feet and found their towels. He tossed one to Andy and struggled to patch the broken bands of his restraint back together as he dried himself. Wordlessly, Andy sat up and ran the towel over her arms and legs. Then she got her brush from her bag and drew it through her wet hair.

By the time he'd finished drying, Joe had full control of himself again. He hoped she hadn't sensed how deeply she had shaken him. Keep it light, he told himself. He dropped on his back beside her and gazed up at the brilliant stars. "You'll never beat me using the breast stroke."

His calm words broke the tension between them. Andy gave a gurgle of laughter. "What should I use then?"

"The crawl."

Lying down on her back, she turned her head to look at him. What was he really thinking, feeling? Was there a part of him that was relieved that she'd had the strength to call a halt? "When did you get into competitive diving?"

"High school. It was a small school, so you didn't have to be very good to make the swim team. And I wasn't very good in the beginning. The coach needed another diver, so I was elected. He told me if I worked hard and was good enough by the time I was a senior, he'd try to get me an athletic scholarship for college. That cinched it. I didn't want my folks to support me through school. They'd have done it if I'd asked, but I didn't want to ask. So I became one of the top high school divers in the state." He turned his head and their gazes met in the moonlight. "Were you in high school sports?"

"Basketball. We had a good girls' team my last two years. Went to the state play-offs when I was a senior, but we got beaten out in the semifinals."

He grinned, imagining her leaping for the basket and dunking the ball in. "Did you go to college?"

"For one year. I wasn't tall enough or good enough to make the team in college. Anyway, I wanted plenty of time to study. I was planning to be a lawyer."

"What happened?"

"Harley happened."

"I see. He swept you off your feet."

She laughed softly. "I was awfully dumb, and Harley was a good-looking guy, two years older than I. He'd dated half the girls on campus before I got there, and a lot of them were still mad about him. When he started paying attention to me, I couldn't get over it. The first two times he took me out, I just sat and stared at him with these worshipful cow eyes, unable to believe my good luck. Harley liked that a lot."

"What man wouldn't?"

"We got married the summer after my freshman year. I worked on campus until he got his degree. Then he went out into the real world and everything changed. Harley wasn't the big man on campus anymore. He could no longer get by on charm alone. Six months was the longest he ever stayed on a job. He always had a good excuse for quitting. Some woman slept with the boss and got promoted over him. The boss's son was brought in and made Harley's life hell because he was jealous. Nobody understood him or appreciated him. I believed him as long as I could, but when he quit the third job I had to accept what was painfully obvious. By the time I realized what a stupid mistake I'd made, I was pregnant with Brad."

"Did you ever think of going home to your parents?"

"Lots of times. But then Tony came along, and my mother became ill. She died when Tony was three. I brought the boys back for the funeral—Harley was off somewhere talking to somebody about investing in a mink farm. After the funeral, I almost told Pop how unhappy I was. But in the end I couldn't do it. Pop had enough problems just then, and I knew the boys needed their father. I told myself Harley would settle down eventually, and things would get better.'' As she talked, Joe's fingers brushed hers. Their hands lay perfectly still, fingertips touching. ''I suppose you think I'm a slow learner,'' Andy said.

''No.'' He gently pressed his fingertips against hers. ''You kept the family together for the children's sake. I can understand that.''

Something in the tone of his voice convinced her that he really did understand. She sighed deeply. ''Thank you. Of course, when things got bad enough, I began to think I was doing the boys more harm than good by staying. I didn't love Harley anymore, but I could have lived with that if it had been the only problem. It was Harley's selfishness that I finally couldn't tolerate. He'd pull the boys out of school two or three times in a year. On the basis of some wild idea that he was convinced would make him rich he'd sell everything we'd managed to accumulate since the last time and move us to another state. The boys reached the point where they were afraid to make friends, because they knew they'd have to leave them. The last straw...''

She stopped, as though the memory were painful. He gazed at her. Her face was so close to his that he could feel her warm breath. It stirred the embers of his banked need. He turned his head and looked up at the sky again. ''What?''

"The last time we moved Brad was nine. We'd been living in Iowa for five months, and he'd had trouble adjusting in school. He hadn't made any friends, so I thought he wouldn't mind moving so much. We loaded everything into a rental van, and I went through the house one last time to make sure we hadn't left anything. Harley had Tony in the van with him. He kept yelling at me to get Brad, that we had to go. Brad had disappeared. I looked around and found him outside, huddled down in the narrow space between the house and the garage. He was just sitting there, crying but not making a sound." She swallowed. "I thought he'd hurt himself. I ran to him and asked what was wrong. He looked at me with tears streaming down his face and said, 'Mom, why can't we be like other people? I hate the way we live!'" She drew in a steadying breath and expelled it slowly. "A week later, I brought the boys back here and moved in next door to Pop."

His fingers crept around hers and squeezed gently. "Have you ever regretted it?"

"Never. I still struggle with guilt feelings sometimes. I get emotional about what growing up without a father will do to the boys, but intellectually I always know I did the right thing."

"Guilt doesn't have much to do with the intellect."

She raised herself up on one elbow to peer at him. All at once his voice had acquired a very grave tone. "You're talking about yourself now, aren't you?"

"Maybe." He shifted and sat up. "When..." He hesitated, as though the words were hard to get out. "When my family was killed, they were on their way to visit Miriam's parents. The trip was my idea, totally mine. The kids didn't want to go, and Miriam wasn't all that excited about it, either. She was no closer to her parents than I was to mine. I talked them into it.''

She watched him pull on his jeans and put away the leftover food and dirty dishes. She couldn't see his face, only movements in the darkness. ''When their plane crashed, you blamed yourself,'' she observed quietly. ''Sometimes you still do.''

He reached for one of the coolers. ''If I hadn't insisted that they go, they'd be alive today.''

She sighed. ''You don't know that.''

At length, he said tersely, ''You're right, I don't.'' He stood over her for an instant, and she sensed that he wanted to say something else, but the moment passed. ''Are you ready to go?''

''Yes. I'll bring the spread and the other cooler.''

By the time they'd put their clothes on over their damp suits and were driving back toward town, the gloom that had descended on Joe had lifted. He reached for her hand and laced his fingers through hers. ''Andy.'' She looked over at him questioningly. ''About what happened tonight,'' he began, then altered his course. ''Would you do something for me?''

''What?''

''We'd be good together. You can't have any doubts about that.''

''No. No doubts,'' she agreed pensively.

''We don't have to deny ourselves what we both want and need. It doesn't have to be complicated unless we want it to be.''

She caught her bottom lip between her teeth. It sounded reasonable when he put it like that. As long as they had an understanding, from the beginning... Andy frowned as she realized that she was gripping his hand more tightly. She relaxed her grip and gazed at his profile. He looked perfectly calm and collected. No complications. Was it possible? He obviously believed it was. They were adults who knew their own minds. Neither of them was prone to acting on whim. Andy tried to shake off a feeling of sadness, wishing she could be as casual as he appeared to be.

He glanced at her with an oddly guarded expression. "Will you think about it at least?"

She hesitated another moment. She would think about every minute of this evening, in any case. "All right," she said. "We can both think about it. Now..." She settled back against the seat. "Tell me exactly how you prepared that trout."

Joe flashed her a grin. He forced down images of Andy clinging to him in the water, her throat arched, her head falling back as though its weight were too much for her. He would deal with his own misgivings later, if at all. "It's easy," he said lightly. "I saw it once on a Saturday morning TV show. What you do is..."

They talked about food until they reached Andy's house. As they got out of the car, Joe said, "What's Bo doing out in the yard this late?"

All the lights in Bo's house, including his porch light, were on. Andy quickened her steps. "There's Brad, too. In his pajamas!" Bo saw them as Andy began to run. "Pop, what's going on?"

Bo put his arm around Brad's shoulders. "Now, Andy, don't get excited."

Her heart clenched. When Bo used that tone, he was very serious indeed. "What is it?"

"Tony. We can't seem to find him."

"Can't find him!" Andy sent a wild look over Bo's front yard. Except for the area near the porch, it lay in deep shadow. Joe put a protective arm around her. "Have you any idea where he could have gone?"

Bo shook his head. "The boys went to bed at ten. I worked on contest entries for an hour. I could kick myself. I should've checked on the boys sooner."

"Don't beat yourself, Pop," Andy said. "Just tell me."

"At eleven, I looked in on them, before getting ready for bed. Tony was gone. He must have slipped out the back way. We've looked all over my house and yours, the yards, too. He's just not here."

"I was asleep, Mom," Brad said. "I didn't know he was gone until Grandpa woke me up."

"His pajamas were on the floor beside the bed," Bo put in.

Andy felt panic gathering in her stomach. "This is insane! He has to be around here somewhere. Come on. We'll search again." She started for her own front steps. Joe followed her.

Behind them, Brad said, "His new backpack's not in his closet, Mom."

Andy whirled around. "Are you sure he didn't leave it somewhere else?"

"It was in his closet this afternoon. I saw it. And he didn't take it to Grandpa's."

"How did he get back into the house? The doors were locked, and Pop has the only other key."

"I had it on my key ring, in my pocket," Bo volunteered.

Brad looked down at his bare feet. "He must have hid it somewhere in the yard before we went to the movie." He looked up. "I think he ran away, Mom."

"Oh, dear God!" While she had been enjoying herself, drinking champagne, swimming, kissing Joe, her child had been going through a major emotional crisis. After the disappointment over the camping trip, she'd left him and gone off with Joe, as though she hadn't a care in the world. Tony must have felt cast-off, deserted. He hadn't known how to deal with those feelings, so he'd run away. "We have to call the police."

"Andy," Joe said, "hadn't we better look a few more places before we do that? He probably hasn't gone far."

"Let's not go off half-cocked," Bo added. "Most kids think about running away sometime. Tony was cross all evening, but I didn't pay that any mind. Maybe he's just trying to get our attention."

Andy twisted her hands together nervously. She thought that was probably the case, but she was still worried. "We can't stand here and do nothing."

"I might know where he's gone," Brad said.

Andy looked at him sharply. "You mean he told you? Why haven't you said something before now?"

"He didn't tell me, Mom. I didn't know he was thinking about running away. It's just that he was really counting on that camping trip with Dad. He got mad at me when I said Dad might be too busy to come. He kept saying over and over that we were going camping.''

"Brad," Andy interrupted impatiently, "what has this to do with where Tony might have gone?"

"We went out to the lake twice to look for camping spots. We found this neat place that Tony really liked. Well . . . you know how he hates to admit it when he's wrong. Do you think he decided to go camping alone?"

Brad's words had the ring of truth. Tony could be stubborn and he had been adamant about the camping trip. "Can you take me there?"

"Yes," Brad said eagerly.

"Hurry and get dressed, then," Andy said. "You can show me where this place is. We'll check it out before we go to the police." Brad ran to Bo's house.

"I'll stay here," Bo said, "in case Tony comes back."

Andy turned to Joe abstractedly, as though she'd just remembered he was there. "Joe . . ."

"I'm going with you," he said firmly.

Andy's hand fluttered to her throat as she realized just how much she wanted to have Joe's strength to lean on until Tony was found. She smiled wanly. "Thank you. I'd appreciate that."

Chapter Ten

I thought he was okay," Andy agonized as Joe drove away from her house. "He didn't seem so depressed today."

"He got mad because you wouldn't let him go with you and Joe tonight," Brad said from the back seat. "He griped about it all the way to the movie. He acted like a brat. Finally Grandpa told him he was spoiling everybody's evening, so he shut up."

Andy scanned the street ahead and on either side of the car, looking for a small figure wearing a backpack. "I wasn't sensitive enough to his needs," she sighed. "I shouldn't have gone out tonight."

Joe gave her a sharp look. "You told your father not to beat himself. Take your own advice, Andy."

"It wouldn't have made any difference, anyway," Brad said, with a wisdom beyond his years. "When he's got his nose out of joint, you have to leave him alone till he gets over it.''

Reaching over her shoulder, Andy patted Brad's hand, which was gripping the back of her seat. He was turning into such a serious, responsible boy, and she must be careful not to expect too much from him. Maybe unconsciously he was trying to take Harley's place in the family. If she'd given him the message that she wanted him to, she must correct it. Brad had adjusted amazingly well to Harley's absence. He was old enough to remember what it was like when they were with his father, and to realize that their life now was an improvement in many ways. Tony, on the other hand, had been only seven when his parents separated. He hadn't been jerked from one school to the next for nearly four years, as Brad had been. He was more inclined to embellish his memories of his father, forgetting Harley's flaws. And she hadn't helped him to see Harley more realistically, Andy mused. She had always thought he was too young, that he would have plenty of time for reality later on.

''Tony's hurting, Brad,'' Andy said finally, ''so he's striking out at us by running away.''

''He's punishing the wrong people,'' Joe muttered.

Andy shot him a confused look. ''Sometimes...well, I'm not always sure I handle Tony in the best way.''

''You have good instincts,'' Joe said. ''It's not that you don't know what to do. It's that you have a hard time being objective when it comes to the people you love.'' He reached for her hand and squeezed it. They were approaching the lake, and Joe asked, "Which road do I take, Brad?"

"Hang a left," Brad said.

Andy was sitting forward in her seat, peering ahead through the windshield. "I can't believe he walked this far. It's three miles."

"My scout troop hiked out here in forty-five minutes once," Brad said. "If Tony left as soon as I went to sleep, he's had an hour."

It was a different road from the one Andy and Joe had taken earlier that evening. It wound away from the lake through thick stands of trees, and at the edge of the road, Andy thought she saw something moving. "Look! What's that?"

The figure ahead was finally overtaken by the reach of the car's headlights. He turned around, squinting, then scurried into the trees.

"It's him!" Brad cried.

Joe braked the car. Andy was out and running the instant the car came to a stop. "Tony!"

"Mom?" The voice held a frightened quaver. Then Tony crept out from behind a bush. As Andy approached, she began to make out his features with the help of a patch of moonlight that filtered down through the trees. He was tired and frightened and wet with perspiration, and he looked as though he'd been crying. A streak of dirt bisected one cheek.

Andy grabbed him and hugged him fiercely. He was trembling. "You had us scared to death, Tony. What on earth got into you?"

"I want to go camping," he muttered against her. He twisted free of her embrace as Joe and Brad came up. He scowled at all three of them. As tired and frightened as he was, he persisted stubbornly, "Dad was supposed to take us camping!"

"Tony," Andy said, straining for patience, "everybody has to learn to handle disappointments. I don't know why your father didn't come. You can ask him the next time he calls. But it's not fair to take it out on the rest of us. You knew that Grandpa wouldn't allow you to come out here alone, so you sneaked off in the middle of the night."

"Grandpa's worried, Tony," Brad put in.

"You must have known we'd all be worried sick when he discovered you were gone."

"Not you," Tony said hotly. "You'd probably be glad to get rid of me. You went out with Joe, and you knew I didn't want to stay with Grandpa tonight."

When had her younger son become so adept at pushing her guilt buttons? Andy wondered and knew she couldn't let him get away with it. "I love you, Tony, but I have needs, too. Joe and I wanted to go out alone tonight, and I will not apologize for that. It's certainly no excuse for running away."

"I didn't run away! I was going camping. I told you!"

Andy felt her temper rising. "Tony, you've misbehaved all weekend, and I'm fed up. Now—"

"You did something to stop Dad from coming!" Tony accused. "I know you did! He promised he'd come, so you must have called him and told him not to. I don't like you anymore!"

"Tony..." Joe stepped forward.

Andy put a warning hand on Joe's arm. "Let me handle this." She gripped Tony's arm and propelled him back to the road. She felt frustrated and unjustly accused, but she knew she might say something she'd regret if she gave her tongue free rein. As they reached the car, she finally managed, "At this moment, I don't like you very well, either, Tony. If I say anything now it'll be the wrong thing, so we'll finish this discussion when we get home."

As they drove to town, the silence in the car was thick and oppressive. Nobody said a word until they reached Andy's house. She turned to Joe. "You don't need to get out. Thank you for helping."

Brad and Tony were already out of the car and walking across the yard. Next door, Bo had come out on his porch. "I'll fill Bo in," Joe said. "What are you going to do?"

"Clear the air." She opened the car door and stepped out. "I'll talk to you later, Joe."

Tony and Brad went directly to their rooms, and Andy went to the kitchen for a drink of water. She stood at the sink and composed herself. She hadn't realized until tonight how much anger Tony had inside of him. Tonight she'd been the target because she was handy. She stood there and tried to understand what Tony was feeling. Harley had disappointed Tony before, but the aborted camping trip had apparently been one disappointment too many. The bad feelings had been building inside Tony until he had to let them out. She realized now that she had contributed to his anger by making excuses for Harley and trying to calm Tony down. What she should have done was say, "I'm sorry your father let you down again. It's okay to be angry. I understand what you're feeling.'' Then he could have gotten rid of it a little at a time instead of all at once, as he had tonight.

Bo was right. She couldn't keep Tony and Brad from being hurt by life. Heaven knew she was weary of trying. Maybe it was time she stopped covering up for Harley. He would have to accept responsibility for his own decisions from now on. She was going to be more open with the boys—she turned away from the sink—and she was going to start now, tonight.

She stuck her head into Brad's room. ''Brad, will you come into Tony's room, please. I want to talk to both of you.''

The red backpack lay on Tony's desk. He had stripped down to his underwear and was sitting on the side of the bed. Brad came in, still in his jeans, and sat beside Tony.

They looked up at Andy, Tony warily, Brad gravely. They're not small boys anymore, Andy reflected with a tiny ache of regret. She pulled a chair away from the desk and sat down, facing them. ''There are some things I've needed to say to you for a long time. I've put it off because I thought I was protecting you. I told myself you were too young to understand. I see now that I was wrong, and I'm sorry.''

Both boys were looking at her with wide, solemn eyes. She went on, ''Tony, Brad, your father loves you. I don't want you to doubt that. But he's not a very responsible person. He makes impulsive promises that he later decides are too much trouble to keep.''

"Then why does he make them?" Tony asked.

"I think he must mean to keep them at the time," Andy said. "Also, he wants people to like him, you boys especially."

The room was quiet for a long moment. Then Tony muttered, "He already knows we like him."

Andy searched for words to explain things that she herself was only coming to understand. "Deep down inside, your father is afraid you'll stop liking him if he tells you no. So he says yes, and then he can't follow through. Tony, I haven't talked to your father since he called and promised to take you camping. I don't even know how to get in touch with him. It hurt me and made me angry when you accused me of telling him not to come this weekend."

Tony stared at his hands. "I—I guess I didn't really mean it."

"I'm doing the best I can to make a home for us," Andy continued. "Don't get me wrong. I'm not bucking for any medals. I like our life, and I like my job. I'm doing exactly what I want to do. I just want to say that I'm not going to take the blame for your father's thoughtlessness. And I'm tired of covering up for him."

Brad looked perplexed. "Covering up—how do you mean, Mom?"

Andy took a deep breath. "Tony, I bought that backpack for you. Your father forgot it was your birthday. He felt bad when I reminded him, but the fact is he forgot." She looked at her older son. "Brad, I doubt that we'll be able to go skiing next winter unless your father sends us some money. He hasn't sent any for six months. I don't think he means to deny you boys anything, but I think he isn't working regularly."

Brad took it calmly, as though he weren't really surprised by her words. Tony looked up at her, his expression miserable, and swallowed hard.

Andy reached for him with her left hand, then took Brad's hand in her right. "Those are examples of what I mean when I say Harley is thoughtless. He's never deliberately unkind. He simply doesn't think much about other people."

"I don't guess he's very grown-up," Brad observed gravely. "I think he'd rather have stayed a kid all his life."

"You may be right, Brad," Andy said.

"He doesn't like to go to work every day," Brad went on.

"He's easily bored," Andy added. "He wants every day to be exciting and different. I guess we'd all like that, but that's not real life. In all fairness, your father has his good points, too. For one thing, he's a lot of fun to be with. People like to be around him because he makes them laugh."

"Sometimes," Tony said in a small voice, "I don't think he loves us at all. If he loves us, why doesn't he come to see us?"

"He does love you, I promise you," Andy said. "But the next time he calls maybe you should tell him how you feel."

"What if he gets mad?" Tony asked.

"One thing about your father, he never stays mad very long. That's another one of his good points."

Tony's hand squeezed hers convulsively. "Mom, I didn't really mean it when I said I didn't like you."

Andy smiled. "Oh, yes, you did. Right then, neither of us liked the other very much. There are going to be times when we don't like the people we love, Tony. That's okay. I know you love me, and I love you." She leaned forward and wrapped her arms around both boys, pulling their heads next to hers on either side. "I love both of you. Very much. That's never going to change. Even when I say no or lose my temper, I still love you." After a moment, she straightened up. "By the way, Tony, you're grounded for a week."

He drew in a deep breath. "I was afraid you were going to say for a month."

She tousled his hair. "It'll be a month if you ever scare me that badly again. That's a promise. Does anybody have anything else to say?"

"Tomorrow," Tony said, "I'll tell Grandpa I'm sorry for worrying him."

"Good," Andy said. "Now, let's hit the sack."

She tucked Tony in and kissed him, then did the same for Brad. In her bedroom, she undressed in the dark and, not taking time to find a nightgown, crawled into bed naked. Yawning, she curled on her side, enjoying the feel of the cool sheets against her bare skin. She'd forgotten how free it felt to sleep nude.

Freedom. It was a concept she hadn't thought about for a while. She was, she reflected, freer than she'd been a few hours earlier. The frank talk with the boys had been liberating. They had taken it well, she mused. It should be easier for them to be honest with each other from now on. Joe was right—it was simpler to live honestly.

Joe. She thought about his earnest gray eyes, his slow smile. For a few minutes at the lake, she'd experienced another kind of freedom. A releasing of inhibitions and restraints. A letting go. But it had happened too fast, and it had frightened her. Joe had been patient and understanding, and he'd been as concerned about Tony as she had been. She wondered drowsily if she'd remembered to thank him.

Andy didn't see Joe for several days, and since Tony was confined to the house for a week, neither did the boys. Andy had three new jobs waiting and she kept so busy that she had time to think of little else until the weekend. Saturday and Sunday she stayed inside with Tony. After a hard week, she had looked forward to a few days of idleness, but she found she couldn't settle in one place for long.

"Mom," Tony asked Sunday afternoon, "why are you so nervous?"

"I've got cabin fever."

"Me, too." Earlier Tony had watched mournfully as Brad left the house with two friends.

"Let's get our minds on something else. How about a game of Monopoly?"

"O-kaay!"

She didn't enjoy the game much, but she managed to give a good enough performance to convince Tony she was having fun. At length she realized what her problem was. She was waiting for a phone call from

Joe. It didn't come, and Sunday night Andy decided to call him. After all, she should let him know how much she appreciated his support the night Tony ran away. She let the phone ring ten times, but there was no answer. Disappointed, she got ready for bed.

She welcomed Monday. It was easier to put Joe out of her mind when she was working. Several days later, on Thursday afternoon, Tony and Brad ran out of Bo's house the minute she turned into the drive.

"Mom! Guess what?" Brad greeted her.

Tony didn't give her time to speak. "We're going camping! We're going camping!"

Andy smiled absently and headed for the house. She was so hot and tired that she unlocked the door and they were inside before Tony's words sank in. She turned to him. "Camping? Did you hear from your father?"

"Nope!" Brad grinned at Tony, who grinned back.

"Is Pop going?"

"Nope," Tony said.

Andy sighed. "I don't think it's a good idea for you to go alone."

"We're not," Brad said.

Andy turned up the air conditioner and sank wearily into a chair. "Look, guys, I'm beat. Don't ask me to play Twenty Questions. Just tell me what you're talking about."

"You tell her," Tony said to Brad.

"Joe's taking us camping," Brad announced.

"Next weekend," Tony added.

"You can come, too," Brad said magnanimously.

"Joe?" Andy sat up straight in her chair, her weariness forgotten. "Who says Joe's taking you camping?"

The boys exchanged confused looks. "Well, Joe did. We saw him in the drugstore today," Tony said.

"Did you ask him to take you?"

"No, Mom, honest," Brad said. "We didn't say a word about it till he brought it up."

"He said he wanted to go camping, but he didn't like to go alone," Tony explained. "So he asked us to go with him."

"Yeah, and then he said we could invite you," Brad put in.

"It's okay, isn't it, Mom?" Tony asked anxiously.

Andy was suddenly very angry. The strength of her reaction surprised her. She got to her feet. "We'll see," she muttered as she headed for the shower.

She stood under the warm shower spray, confused and fuming. How dare Joe plan a camping trip with the boys without asking her permission first! He could have picked up the phone any time in the past ten days and talked to her about it, but he hadn't. He'd let Brad and Tony spring it on her without warning. If she nixed the plans now, she'd be the villain in her sons' eyes. How could Joe have put her in this position?

She rinsed the soap from her body and stepped out on the mat. She grabbed a towel and dried hurriedly. She wasn't going to fume in silence. Be honest, Joe had said. Well, by heaven, she'd be honest then. She'd tell him exactly what she thought of his high-handedness.

Dressed in shorts, shirt and sandals, she warmed dinner in the microwave and set it on the table. "I have to go out for awhile," she told the boys. "Brad, you're in charge. I won't be gone long."

She drove to Joe's house, and she saw that his car was in the drive. She pulled in behind it, went to the door and knocked impatiently.

From somewhere in the house, Joe yelled, "Be there in a minute."

It was, in fact, several minutes before he opened the door, dressed in jeans and a white T-shirt. He had obviously come directly from the shower. His hair was still damp and mussed from drying it with a towel. His eyes lit up at the sight of her.

Before he could say anything she pushed past him and into the living room. Hands on her hips, she demanded, "What do you think you're doing?"

He contemplated her angry stance. Then he closed the door and lounged against it. "You mean right now, this minute?"

"You know damned well what I mean!" she countered.

He straightened slowly and came toward her. He cupped her chin in his hands. "What's wrong?"

Andy stepped away so that he was no longer touching her. "Stop that!" Her nerves were suddenly tingling from his touch. "You know perfectly well what's wrong. I came home this afternoon and learned you'd had the colossal gall to plan a camping trip without saying anything about it to me. Not one word! How dare you—!"

"Andy." Joe cut her off. "I told them they'd have to get your permission."

"Oh, that's just wonderful." Biting back her fury, she stomped away from him, then whirled back to face him. "Now if I say no, I'm the bad guy." She shook her head. "I can't believe you'd do this to me."

Frowning, he walked across the room, narrowing the space between them to inches. "It seemed like a good idea at the time. They were so elated about going camping with Harley, and then he didn't come.... Well, there's no reason they can't have their camping trip, anyway, is there?"

"That's not the point," she said in a trembling voice that told her, and him, just how upset she was. "The point is that you decided, without my knowledge, to step in and save the day." She stared at him and added deliberately, "You are not their father. You have no right to make any plans involving my sons without my permission. You're taking advantage of their disappointment in Harley. And you've put me in the position of having to agree to the camping trip or disappoint them again."

She saw hurt in his eyes, along with a flare of temper that he was obviously trying to control. "You're right," he said flatly, surprising her. "I'm not their father. I should have talked to you about the trip first." His voice was calm and patient, but his eyes were tumultuous. The late afternoon sun coming through the venetian blinds fell in bars across his face. Andy was suddenly, electrically, aware of the tension in the room.

"That doesn't help much at this point. I still have to go home and give them an answer."

He cocked his head. "Do you have other plans for the weekend?"

"No."

"Then why is it such a difficult decision? You might actually enjoy it."

"I'm sure of it." Her own words astonished her. She stared at him, confused, then ran an agitated hand through her hair.

"I see." He took a step toward her. All at once, the tight dread in his chest eased. "This isn't about the boys, is it? You're afraid to spend the weekend with me. That's what this is about."

"No, I . . ." She took a step back. "I'm not afraid. That's ridiculous." But the disclaimer sounded hollow. "I—I have to go. . . ."

Joe matched his steps to hers. "Why, Andy?" He lifted his hand and touched her cheek. She stood still. "Why are you so afraid of me?"

She knew there was no point in denying it again. "Because," she blurted, "I don't want to fall in love with you." She drew in an astounded breath and pressed the fingers of one hand against her mouth as though to erase the words.

"Why?" he asked simply, his hand resting lightly on her face, his eyes intent.

"I can't be as casual as you are. You said we could have an affair without complications. Maybe you can, but I'm not capable of it." Her look was filled with dismay at the truths that were spilling from her lips. "I simply can't."

Taking his time, he let his fingers caress her cheek and then her throat. "Maybe I'm incapable of it, too," he said quietly. "I can't know—we can't know the end before we've even made a beginning."

She gave him a penetrating look. If she wasn't careful, he would seduce her with soft, reasoned arguments, she thought, and felt a flutter of panic. She couldn't debate him. "I might be willing to risk it," she faltered, "if—if you weren't still grieving for your wife. Miriam is between us, Joe. Perhaps she would always be."

She saw a flare of something in his eyes—pain? shock? anger? His hand cupped the back of her neck, his fingers holding her immobile. "You don't know what you're talking about." His other hand traced down her cheek. "I grieve for Miriam because she was the mother of my children and because she deserved more than she got out of her short life."

"I don't understand," she whispered, wondering if he could feel the pounding of her heart.

"I wasn't in love with Miriam."

He said it so quietly that it was a moment before she understood. Then she stiffened. "Don't lie to me, Joe. Please, don't."

He lifted a brow. "I've never lied to you."

Her thoughts were a mass of confusion. "But you gave up diving for her. You—you were married to her for years. She loved you."

"Yes, she loved me." He stopped, as though the words were painful for him. "But that wasn't why I stayed in the marriage. The children were everything to me. I didn't want their lives disrupted. I couldn't bear the thought of being separated from them."

He hadn't loved Miriam. Why did this revelation frighten her so? "I always thought..." Her voice trailed off as his fingers massaged the tight muscles at the back of her neck.

"It was convenient for you to think so," he murmured. "It provided an excuse to keep me at a distance." He gave her a slow smile. "There are no more excuses, Andy," he said and lowered his mouth to hers.

The kiss shook her like a bolt of lightning. It was hard and possessive, without being frantic or hurried. It was as though he knew he'd demolished her last defense and that there was no fight left in her. I could push him away, she thought fleetingly. I can still tell my hands what to do, and I can lift them to his shoulders and push. But the desire to do so was missing. Andy felt the last shreds of the outrage that had brought her to Joe's house oozing out of her. Fear and nervous tension went with it. What was left was a lovely feeling of rightness. This had been fated to happen from the first time they'd met, and she hadn't the strength or the will to deny it any longer. There were other wants rising in her, stronger ones.

Sensing her surrender, Joe lifted his head to look deeply into her eyes. "I need you, Andy."

She saw the passion and the tenderness in his face. The combination made her giddy. I love you, Joe. The words were suddenly clear in her mind, and she accepted the utter truth of them. The knowledge was too new, too fragile, to risk exposing, so she said, "I need you, too, Joe."

Then he lifted her, and her arms were around him, her face pressed against his neck in a gesture not of defeat, but of trust. He vowed to handle her vulnerable heart with exquisite care.

He held her close for a moment, then carried her to his bed. He lowered her and stood looking down at her, his eyes touched with a kind of wonder. "You are so beautiful."

She sighed and lifted her hands to cup his face. "I think I've wanted you to make love to me forever," she murmured as she pulled his mouth down to hers.

Chapter Eleven

Beyond the bedroom windows, the dying sun streaked the western horizon with glorious splashes of red and purple, a vision of fire and opulence. Inside, Andy and Joe were finding their own burning fire.

They didn't speak. Words were unnecessary. Andy suspected that words might intrude jarringly into the rich, dreamy experience that she'd imagined for weeks, but had been sure could never be translated into reality.

Joe's hands were in her hair, and for a moment, she felt them trembling. She found the sensation unbearably exciting. His mouth, wet and hot, roamed her face. Lassitude flowed through her, and with a whispered sigh, she closed her eyes. The bed smelled of him, she thought. His scent lingered in the sheets. It was clean, male, vital. A scent that, as long as she lived, she would never forget.

His mouth was no longer pressing moist kisses on her face, and her dreaminess ebbed for a moment. She opened her eyes. He was looking down at her, his gray eyes darkened by arousal. The light in the room was softened by the coming dusk, and shadows were everywhere. Shadows touched the hollows of his eyes and cheeks. Shadows were long on the pale walls and carpet. Shadows muted everything, wrapping the room in privacy. He continued to stare down at her, as though he wanted to burn her image in his brain. Andy waited, expecting him to speak.

But there was only the hushed silence. Not the silence of emptiness but the silence of awe. Like the quiet in a cathedral, Andy mused. There was something else in the way he watched her, something intense and unwavering. Then she understood. When they'd entered the bedroom, they had left indecision behind. Bridges had been burned, and Andy had no desire to rebuild them. Yet she wondered what dangers she would face because of walking through that door. Her fingers shook as she raised them to his face to trace his jaw and chin and mouth.

Joe laid his hand over hers, stilling the restless movement. Andy smiled at him, a smile that hid a sudden thrill of nerves. Would he find the reality as pleasing as the expectation?

He held her hand loosely on the pillow and studied her. He wanted to remember everything about this moment. He wanted to be able to close his eyes a week, a year from now, and see her hair spread over the pillow in an auburn halo. He wanted to be able to conjure up her face with the shadows caressing it, her lips soft and parted, her expression with its traces of uncertainty and her eyes intent and as deep as midnight with desire.

Then, slowly, he loosed the top button of her shirt and lowered his head. Her eyes fluttered closed, and her warm breath whispered from her mouth in a little moan of anticipation. With exquisite care, he kissed her forehead and then the delicate arch of an eyebrow. Eyes closed, he tasted the curve of one cheek and then the other. He traced the line of her jaw with tiny, feathery kisses, and he breathed in the sweet, feminine scent of her. He kissed the hollow at the base of her throat.

Whimpering a soft plea, Andy turned her head, her mouth searching for his. But he prolonged the agony, his thumb settling in the faint indentation above her upper lip, then following the bottom one with gentle strokes. His mouth continued to beguile and promise as it flowed over her face and throat, stopping frequently to nibble and taste.

A shudder of pleasure escaped her parted lips as he planted open-mouthed kisses at each corner of her mouth. With a moan, she tugged his T-shirt from his jeans and molded her hands to the muscles of his lower back. Her fingers gripped convulsively, then restlessly moved to explore him.

Her eager response sent a wild surge of excitement through Joe. He wanted to feel her passion, to know that the fire in her raged as high as his own. He clamped down on the frantic urge to satisfy his burgeoning hunger with haste. Patience, he told himself. Savor every nuance. He brought his mouth to hers, and the tip of his tongue traced her lips and entered her mouth. She groaned, and her arms wrapped around his neck. Without warning, their passion exploded. His lips crushed hers, and her tongue hungrily explored the interior of his mouth. The shadows lengthened, and the sound of their breathing between fevered kisses was suddenly loud in the quiet bedroom.

Andy tugged at his shirt and whispered breathlessly, "Let me take this off." For a moment, she relaxed her grip as his mouth ravaged hers. "Let me take everything off," she managed finally. "I want to see you."

After another hot, lingering kiss, he rolled over on his back and looked up at her with desire-glazed eyes. She bent over him and he raised his arms as she pulled the shirt over his head. She tossed it on the floor and her fingers worked at the waistband of his jeans, unsnapping and then unzipping. Suddenly remembering his shoes, she untied them and slipped them off, then the socks. Watching her, he raised his hips from the bed, and she worked his jeans down his legs, then pulled them off and tossed them after his shirt. He wore nothing but a pair of white briefs now, and she sat back on her heels to study him.

Her glance paused to take in the mat of dark hair on his chest, the hint of another above his briefs and finally the evidence of his arousal. He watched color rise on her face. With a slow smile, he asked, "Not losing your nerve, are you?"

The flush suffused her cheeks. "No," she whispered. "I was admiring you. You're beautiful." Then her fingers hooked over his briefs and she pulled them off. A sigh rushed from her, and her gaze raked his body and came to rest on his mouth.

"My turn," he said huskily. He sat up and pressed her down on her back. Kneeling beside her, he finished unbuttoning her shirt, peeled it off and threw it over his shoulder. Her sandals went next and then her shorts. He kissed the hollow of her stomach, making her suck in her breath, and then slipped off her panties and bra.

For a long moment, he simply gazed at her. He reached out and cupped his hand over her breast. Then his fingers traced the line of her ribs, the narrow waist, the flat stomach, the jut of a hipbone. "My God," he muttered hoarsely, "you're exquisite." Andy could bear it no longer, and her burning need wrenched a deep moan from her. Desperate for the feel of his flesh against hers, her hands clutched at him.

"Slowly," he muttered, then stretched out beside her and urged her against him with one hand at her waist. Her breasts were crushed against his chest, her stomach and thighs pressed his. He kissed her long and lingeringly.

She could feel the tensing of his muscles as he controlled the need to hurry. His mouth was hard and demanding, then soft and tender. Drunk with passion, she abandoned herself to his lead. Her hands explored his shoulders, his arms and then his rib cage in sensual slow motion. Anticipation rippled over her heated skin.

He raised himself on one elbow, and his gaze burned over her flesh. "I need to look at you." Then he lowered his head and nuzzled her breasts. His tongue flipped over a nipple, bringing it to instant hardness, and he took it into his mouth. A storm of passion mounted as his mouth searched out the secrets of her body.

She would have rushed headlong to completion, but he held her back, gentling her with whispered words. He cooled her heated skin with kisses and eased her back into calmness with slow, soothing hands. He set a deliberately languorous pace until Andy felt as though her very bones were melting.

Joe's hands flowed over her soft, faintly moist skin. She moved restlessly beneath his touch, moaning softly, exciting him to an urgent pitch that took all of his will to keep in check. He wanted to savor, he reminded himself. As he kissed her throat, his hands became familiar with the shape of her shoulders and breasts, the nipples that strained against his palm, the curve of her waist, the long, smooth line of her thighs.

She was firm and soft at the same time, and it almost drove him wild. "So sweet," he murmured while his finger traced her inner thigh. Then he bent over her, allowing his mouth to follow his hands in their exploration. She buried her fingers in his hair and arched against him.

His slow pace was driving her crazy with need. She wanted to feel the full weight of his body over hers, to feel his mouth hard and devouring on hers. Her heartbeat throbbed, loud and fast, in her ears. Every nerve in her body quivered with raw need. Desire as

primitive as the earth ripped through her. Seeking,
demanding assuagement, she wound her arms around
him and, with the power of desperation, pulled him
hard against her.

Joe knew the moment his control snapped. Gentle-
ness fled. The slow, measured pace he had set abruptly
quickened. She was all hunger and fire beneath him.
Unconsciously, his hands became rough on her soft
skin and his mouth became bruisingly insistent. His
breathing was ragged and labored.

Feeling his control breaking, Andy reveled in her
woman's power. Her restless hands molded to his lean
hips with searing urgency. She did not want gentle-
ness. There could be no more waiting. Now—oh,
please now.... Andy didn't know whether she said the
words or only thought them.

It didn't matter. Joe had only one thought, to lose
himself in her. With a single, smooth movement, he
entered her. For a moment, he remained poised, still.
She was tight at first, and then incredibly sweet. He
moved then, and through a daze he heard a cry. Had
the sound come from him? Andy? Both of them?
Then she found his rhythm, and his mouth crushed
hers. They moved as one, slowly at first, but soon
faster.

The eruption, when it came, was wrenching, stunning, and the aftershocks seemed to go on endlessly.
The lovers gave themselves up to sensation.

Dusk lay beyond the windows now. Her hand rested
lightly on the hard curve of his shoulder. Her head
nestled in the hollow of his neck. Their legs were

twined together and entangled in the sheet. Andy sighed. Never had she felt so content. Her body was leaden, and she didn't think she could move if she tried.

Joe's hand stroked her breast. She could still hear his heart pounding, but not as frantically as before. What was it he had said in the living room? *We can't know the end before we've even made a beginning.* Well, they'd made a beginning—what a beginning. They couldn't go back to the way it was before, no matter what happened now. All avenues of escape were barred. Scary thought. Andy shivered.

"You okay?" Joe drew her closer to him, settling his cheek against her hair.

"A little more than okay."

He laughed and caressed the curve of her hip. "Hmmm, I know what you mean." He kissed the top of her head. "You're wonderful, Andy."

"You're pretty great yourself." She strove to keep her voice light. Struggling half-upright, she gazed down into his face. His eyes were gentle. Giving in to impulse, she rained light kisses on his face.

When she lifted her head, he smiled. "Can you stay a while?"

She heaved a sigh. "I'd love to." She relaxed against him again and buried her face against his throat. "But I have to go. I told the boys I'd be back soon. They'll be wondering what's happened."

Her words hung in the air, and his arm tightened around her. "I'm wondering the same thing. What has happened, Andy?"

I've fallen in love with you, she thought, but she couldn't say the words. She didn't know how he felt about her. She couldn't offer her heart without some indication that this fragile new love was not completely one-sided. To say, I love you, was an invitation for the other person to say it, too. If it happened that way, she wasn't sure she could believe him. She had to move, get out of Joe's bed, give them both time and space to think.

She forced herself to pull away from him. "Good question. When you figure out the answer, let me know." She got out of bed and, with quick movements, began to dress.

He watched her, still feeling the weight of her head on his shoulder, the shape of her body wound with his. He had a sharp feeling of loss. "Andy?"

She buttoned her shirt and sat down on the side of the bed to buckle on her sandals. "Yeah?"

He wanted to say that she was beautiful and special and that he thought he was falling in love with her, but her sudden detachment bewildered him. Maybe they both needed more time to get used to what had happened.

"Are we going camping next weekend?"

She gave a weak laugh and stood. "Do I really have a choice?" Before she knew what he was going to do, his hand snaked out, grasped her arm and tugged. She tumbled atop him. "Joe—" He silenced her with a kiss. She allowed herself to relax against him for a moment, then wriggled away again. On her feet once more, she looked down at him. With a shake of her head, she said, "Yeah, I guess we're going camping."

She smiled and walked to the bedroom door. As she went out, she murmured, "It should be an interesting weekend."

They left Saturday morning at the crack of dawn. Andy had packed food and cooking utensils for two days. Joe had borrowed a tent, a two-burner butane stove and two extra sleeping bags from a co-worker. Brad and Tony had their own. They drove to the spot Tony had been heading for the night he ran away. It was a small clearing deep in the woods with a seven-foot outcropping of rock on one side, where they would be sheltered from any wind that penetrated the woods. By the time they'd pitched the tent and set out the stove and utensils it was after eight.

Once they'd set up camp, Andy spread a quilt on the ground and flopped down on her back. She gazed at the lush leaves and the scattered patches of blue sky above her. She inhaled the rich odors of earth and growing things. She watched two redbirds flit from an oak tree to a tree deeper in the woods, fussing at the campers for intruding in their world. She hadn't camped out overnight since she was a child. She'd forgotten the pure, simple pleasure of it.

"This is my idea of heaven," she mused.

"It is, huh?" Joe sat down beside her. He brushed a stray hair out of her face, his fingers lingering for a moment on her skin. Then he glanced at the boys, who were rummaging in a grocery sack for granola bars, removed his hand reluctantly and looped his arms around his bent knees. "I'll tell you my idea of heaven later," he added in a low voice and grinned wickedly.

Their eyes met and held for a moment. Joe's words evoked memories of making love in his bed, and Andy felt her cheeks heat. He had come to her house Friday evening to make plans for the camp-out, but they had been alone only briefly when Andy walked him to his car. Their good-night kiss had been unsatisfactory because Tony kept calling from the house for Andy to come and help him find his canteen. Now they were going to spend two days in each other's company, probably without ever being alone. Andy decided it could be a frustrating weekend. She determined not to let it be.

She sat up. "Okay, gang, time to plan our day. What's first on the agenda?"

"Let's go for a hike," Tony suggested as he tore the wrapping off a granola bar.

"I'd rather go fishing first," Brad said. He had already finished his first bar and was reaching for another.

"I want to swim sometime today," Tony added.

"I don't suppose I could just lie here and nap while you guys do all that other stuff," Andy said.

"No way!" Three voices in unison.

Andy grinned. "I didn't really think so. Well, shall we take a vote or what?"

"If I may make a couple of suggestions," Joe put in. "First we dig for worms. Then we walk to the lake, carrying our poles and bait. It's over a mile, there and back, so we'd get a hike in as well as fishing for something to eat at lunch. We can swim this afternoon."

"Sounds good to me," Andy said, "all except the digging for worms part."

"Everybody digs," Joe insisted.

"What a hard-nose," Andy grumbled.

Joe winked at her over the boys' heads. Then he produced a shovel from the trunk of his car. Within fifteen minutes, they had a bucketful of dirt and earthworms. Tony tossed granola bars and four apples into his backpack and strapped it on. Carrying their fishing poles, they set off for the lake.

Andy loved the crunching sound of dead leaves beneath their feet, the way the sun fell through the trees and dappled her arms, and the boys' irrepressible laughter as they ran ahead, then circled back to show her and Joe an interesting rock or weird-looking insect. Why hadn't she thought of taking the boys camping before this? But somehow she didn't think it would be the same without Joe. Andy watched Brad and Tony vie for his attention. He knew the names of the strange insects they found, and he answered their endless questions without ever seeming to lose patience. He was a natural-born family man.

As they neared the lake, Joe asked, "Hey, anybody know any good knock, knock jokes?"

They'd told every joke they knew by the time they found a good spot on the lake bank and baited their hooks.

"Time to get serious," Joe said.

"Unless we want bologna sandwiches for lunch," Andy joked.

"Ugh!" Tony grimaced and passed out the apples.

They spread out to fish. Brad and Tony walked away in opposite directions and tossed their lines into the water several hundred yards on either side of Andy and Joe, who sat within touching distance of each other. Joe threw his line out and propped his pole against his knee. Leaning back on one elbow, he bit into his apple and watched Andy settle on the grass.

She set her apple aside for later and smiled at him. "You're good with kids."

A hint of a grin played on his mouth. "You're good, too," he countered and wiggled his eyebrows in a terrible imitation of Groucho Marx.

His double entendre made her shake her head. "I can see I'm going to have to be on my toes with you all weekend."

"I'd rather have you on your—"

"Don't say it." She laughed. "Impossible man."

He reached for her free hand, and they sat, their fingers linked, contentedly watching their corks bob on the water. The only sound was Joe munching on his apple.

"I just realized something," Andy said. "You haven't had a cigarette all morning."

"I thought you'd never notice. Tony saw a film on smoking at school, and he told me how my lungs looked. 'All sludged up and full of holes,' is how he put it."

Andy chuckled.

"I decided to quit. I don't want to set a bad example for the kids."

"I'm glad," Andy said, trying not to feel hurt that it had been Tony, instead of her, who'd convinced him.

They caught five bass before they headed back to camp. Joe cleaned the white fish while Andy mixed

batter for hush puppies. It was almost three o'clock by
the time they sat down, paper plates piled with crisp,
golden fish fillets, hush puppies and the coleslaw Andy
had brought packed in ice. Nothing had ever tasted so
good before, they all agreed. They ate with melted
butter dripping off their fingers, glorying in the mess,
and complimenting each other profusely on their
catch.

After stuffing themselves, Joe said, "We'll sink like
rocks if we go in the water now."

They decided to stretch out on quilts for a nap before driving to the lake to swim.

Andy was awakened later by a rumble of thunder.
She yawned and stretched and squinted at her watch.
It was six o'clock. They'd slept nearly three hours! She
sat bolt upright as she heard another peal of thunder.
A giant raindrop plopped on her arm. The patches of
sky that she could see were a dismal dark gray. The
clearing was dim, and the smell of rain was strong in
the air.

She shook Tony, who slept beside her. "Everybody
up. It's going to rain. We have to get everything in the
tent." She grabbed an armload of pots and pans and
ran for shelter, calling, "Come on, you sleepy-
heads!"

Groaning and protesting, Joe and the boys finally
came awake enough to realize what was happening.
Grabbing everything in sight, they raced inside as rain
began to fall in earnest.

They spread the quilts on the canvas floor of the
tent and listened to the rain drumming loudly on the
canvas.

"No swimming today," Tony moaned.

"What if the rain doesn't stop soon?" Brad asked morosely. "We could be stuck in this tent till morning."

Tony flopped down on his back. "Bor-ing."

"Think of this as an adventure," Andy advised. She crawled to where the sleeping bags were piled and reached into hers. "Voilà!" She held up a pack of cards. "We'll play hearts."

They played until it was too dark to see, at which point Joe suggested they tell ghost stories. That and a snack of cookies and canned cola occupied them until bedtime. The boys, who'd drunk two cans each, had to leave the tent twice to relieve themselves. Fortunately the rain had finally stopped. Andy lay in her sleeping bag in an old pair of shorts and a knit shirt and listened to the sound of water dripping off the leaves.

They had arranged the sleeping bags so that Andy's and Joe's were on either side, with the boys' between. During Brad and Tony's second trip outside, Joe moved over and touched Andy's hair in the dark. "Having fun?" His hand stroked down her back.

She stretched under his hand. "Uh-huh. You?"

He kneaded her shoulders, relaxing the muscles. "I haven't enjoyed anything so much in ages."

She knew that giving the boys a good time was a big part of Joe's enjoyment. The thought troubled her a bit, and she flicked it away. She let out a quiet sigh. "We shouldn't have let them drink so much pop," she murmured. "They'll be walking over us half the night."

Joe chuckled and stroked her cheek. "Once they do get to sleep, we could slip out and go skinny-dipping." He said, his voice more teasing than serious.

Andy reached for his hand and brought it to her lips. Smiling, she kissed his palm. "Sounds wonderful, but we couldn't. They might wake up and find us gone."

"You're right," he agreed sadly. He lay on his back beside her. She raised her head to peer down at him. In the dark, she could only make out the suggestion of features. He reached up and cupped her face in his hands, then, groping a little in the dark, kissed her. "It's going to be a restless night," he said, "knowing you're so close and not being able to touch you."

"For me, too."

His hands slipped into her sleeping bag, found her bare midriff and gathered her close. "When am I going to see you alone?"

"I've been thinking about that," she said on an impulse that surprised her. "The boys are sleeping over with friends Tuesday. Can I lure you to my house that night?"

He grinned and gave her a hard, hot kiss. "If you try very hard, and throw in dinner."

She touched his face. "You drive a tough bargain, Underwood."

He chuckled, and they heard the boys running back to the tent over the wet ground. "If I play hard to get, maybe you'll appreciate me more," he said, then scooted back to his side of the tent.

"After this weekend, how can I not appreciate you?"

"Actions speak louder than words," he challenged.

"I'll show you Tuesday night." She settled her head on her folded arms. "Pleasant dreams," she whispered.

A moment later, the boys lifted the tent flap, stepped inside, took off their shoes, and fell against each other as they fumbled and crawled into their bags.

"Ouch," Tony yelped. "You stepped on my finger, Big Foot."

"Be quiet!" Brad hissed. "I think they're asleep."

In the dark, Andy and Joe smiled.

Chapter Twelve

The table in the center of the living room was spread with a yellow linen cloth that swept the floor. Andy's good china and silver, unused since her move to Neptune, gleamed in the flickering light of four candles, which were situated in strategic nooks and crannies. Only the soft light reached the table, not the heat of the flames. A bottle of Chablis rested in an ice bucket on the sideboard. Beside the bucket, two stemmed glasses waited, their bowls reflecting twin flames from the nearest candle.

Andy had stayed up late the previous night, preparing chicken cacciatore with vermicelli and a summer squash casserole. Fifteen minutes before Joe's expected arrival, she had popped the meal into the oven to warm. Now, as she set individual spinach salads on the table, a knock sounded at the door. She spun around, and her floor-length caftan swirled about her legs as she went to answer.

Bo had given her the caftan the previous Christmas—a flowing garment of an expensive soft blue cotton with hot-pink hand-embroidered flowers lining the deep vee of the neckline. Andy had been surprised by the extravagant gift and deeply grateful, though she had wondered when she would ever have an occasion to wear it. She had stored it in a zippered garment bag, and she hadn't taken it out until tonight.

She swung the door open. Joe's gaze lingered for a moment on her flushed face, then raked downward appreciatively as he stepped inside. Andy did some appreciating of her own as she noted the finely tailored, oatmeal-colored sports jacket worn with soft olive green slacks and an olive-and-oatmeal open-collared shirt.

An odd shyness seemed to fall on them as they gazed at each other. Joe's slow grin acknowledged it as he broke the electric contact to glance over the room. "Are we alone?"

"Quite alone. Come into my parlor," Andy quipped and indicated the ice bucket. "Why don't you pour the wine?"

He pulled the wine bottle from its bed of ice and examined the label. "Nice." He popped the cork and poured, then handed her one of the glasses. "What smells so good?"

"You'll see." She sipped her wine while keeping her gaze steady on his.

"Mystery," he murmured and sent another look over the candlelit room. "Hmmm. Wine, food, candles." His eyes came back to hers. "And a beautiful lady. I hope this is what it looks like, beautiful lady."

"Which is?"

"A seduction scene."

She gave him a slow smile. "Would that shock you?"

"It would delight me." He would have touched her then, but she spun away from him.

"Shall we sit down?"

Lifting a brow, Joe followed her to the table and held her chair. He bent to murmur near her ear, "In a teasing mood, are we?"

"Maybe." Andy set down her glass and watched him lower himself into the chair across from her, a smile playing over her lips. She had planned this evening carefully. She meant to explore the limits of her strength, and the depth of his trust. This time she wouldn't be led; she would set the pace. She picked up her salad fork and began to eat.

After a moment, she said, "There are a couple of things I'd like to get out of the way if you don't mind talking about your past."

He studied her carefully. "About my marriage?"

She nodded. "If you'd rather not, just say so."

"No, it's all right." He got up to fetch the bottle and refill their glasses. "What is it you want to know?"

She touched the rim of her glass. "When did you stop loving Miriam? What happened to make you stop?"

He ate another bite of his salad before he replied. "Nothing happened." He sat back and gazed at her. "How can I explain it to you?" He took a sip of wine. "I was twenty-one when I got married. I'd come out of this undemonstrative, cold family background, where I knew I was never really wanted. Miriam wanted me. More than that, she wanted what I wanted.''

"A family," Andy murmured.

He nodded. "She represented what I'd never had, and I was fond of her, loved her, I suppose, in a way. I just wasn't in love with her. By the time I stopped to think about the difference, we had two children.''

"So you made the children the center of your life,'' Andy said, as much to herself as to him.

Again, he nodded. "Eventually Miriam knew something was wrong. She said she felt me slipping away from her. It terrified her. She turned into a mass of insecurities, demanding and clinging by turns. It was...difficult to take, day after day. I knew I'd have asked for a divorce if we hadn't had children, and that made me feel guilty as hell.''

Andy saw the same flicker of pain in his eyes that she'd noticed the evening they met.

He took a deep breath. "So, I said she was imagining things, that we'd just let the marriage get stale, that what we needed was a little time apart. I suggested that she take the kids to visit her family for a few weeks. She didn't want to go. Somehow she'd convinced herself that I was having an affair and wanted her out of the way. I wasn't, by the way, but I desperately needed some time alone. After which, I'd convinced myself, I would be able to make a fresh commitment to the marriage. I didn't know how I was going to accomplish that; all I knew was that I couldn't leave Miriam without leaving the children, and I wasn't willing to do that." He reached for his wineglass and drained it. "I lost them anyway."

His voice was expressionless, but Andy knew that there were painful emotions buried inside him. She had reflected frequently on his earlier revelation that he hadn't loved Miriam, but for some reason she had needed to be reassured. Now she wished she'd left it alone. "I'm sorry. I have no right...."

He looked at her intently. "You have a right," he said simply. "I care very deeply for you and your boys, Andy. I think you know that."

Yes, she had always known that the boys were a part of the package. What she didn't know was how much Joe cared for her apart from her sons. This wasn't the first time he'd made her aware that Brad and Tony were filling the void left in his life by the loss of his children. If she were childless, would Joe be here this very minute? That was a question she couldn't answer. She wondered if Joe himself could answer it, and this was not the time to ask. She rose and removed their salad plates. "I'll be back in a minute with dinner."

For the remainder of the meal, she steered the conversation away from the past. She asked about Bo's commercial, and Joe said the results coming in from the test markets looked strong. The powers that be would make a decision in September about showing it nationwide. They talked about Bo and his domino-playing cronies, laughing over some of Andy's memories of them, from when she was growing up. By the time they'd finished the meal and emptied the bottle of wine, the atmosphere between them was light and easy.

"Let's sit on the couch," Andy suggested, then took his hand and led him there. When she would have released his hand, he held on and pulled her against him with the intention of kissing her as he'd been dying to do all evening.

But she tilted her head back, keeping her lips inches from his. "There's another bottle of wine in the refrigerator. Shall I get it?"

"Don't you move."

With a low laugh, she slid her hands up the front of his jacket, pushing it off his shoulders. When she felt his arms come around her, she nibbled lightly on his bottom lip, then pulled back to undo the first button of his shirt. "I'll put some music on," she murmured and slipped from his arms.

As she crossed to the tape storage cabinet in the corner of the room, Andy stepped out of her shoes. She slipped a medley of romantic show tunes into the player and turned the volume low. Then she circled the room, blowing out candles.

Joe watched the seductive way her gown moved against her body, watched her turn toward him and slowly lift her thick auburn hair with her hands, then let it fall.

"I think," he said quietly, "that we're finally getting to the evening's highlight."

With a sound that was half laugh, half sigh, Andy walked back to him. "You didn't think my dinner was a highlight?"

"What dinner?"

Grinning, she settled onto a corner of the couch and pulled him toward her. "The dinner I slaved over half the night," she said, nipping at his ear.

"Oh, that dinner. I remember it vaguely." With a swift movement of his head, his mouth captured hers.

She relaxed against him for the briefest moment, then broke the kiss. "I'm so glad." She ran her fingers through his hair. "I would hate to have done all that work for nothing."

"Are we about to have dessert?" Joe reached out to cup the back of her head and pull her closer.

Andy caught his hand in hers. "Yes, but don't be greedy. Dessert is so much better if you take it slowly." She turned his hand over and pressed a moist kiss in the palm. She traced his lifeline with a fingernail, then turned his hand over again to stroke the few dark hairs above the knuckles. "Have I ever told you that I like your hands?"

"No." He was watching her, mesmerized.

She kissed the inside of his thumb. "They're strong." She kissed the pad of his index finger. "And so clever. I love it when your hands touch my skin." She pressed his palm against her cheek.

Joe stared at her as hot fingers of desire licked through his blood. Around them flowed the whispered words of a love song, and her low voice seemed somehow a part of the music. In the dim light, her eyes looked dark and languid. "Andy..."

"Shh." She placed a finger against his mouth. "I haven't finished. Let me see, I've told you how much I like your hands. I like your hair, too. Especially the way it curls here, over your ear." She combed through the curls in question with her fingers. "You have a nice face, too. It's masculine and—now, don't let this go to your head, but I find you terribly handsome." She ran the tip of her finger over one eyebrow, then traced a cheekbone. "Lovely mouth, so exciting and sexy." She smoothed the pad of her finger over his bottom lip, watching the movement intently. Then she brushed her lips over his. "Do you remember the first time you kissed me? It knocked me out. Afterward, I thought about it all the time. I couldn't get over it."

When she would have shifted away from him, he reached out with both hands and cupped her head. "Andy." His voice was low and husky with desire. "Come here."

He brought his mouth down to hers and kissed her deeply. Andy fought the temptation to give in to the languor that seemed to be taking over her body. She let her head fall back against the couch, evading his tongue. "Tsk, tsk, you are a greedy man."

"Temptress," he muttered. "Witch." He met her challenging look and bent to kiss the arch of her throat. "Your taste makes me crazy. Your scent drives me wild."

Sighing, Andy undid another one of his shirt buttons and slid her hands inside, feeling the rough mat of chest hair and the deep pounding of his heart. "Easy," she whispered. "Tell me more."

He tangled his fingers in her hair, lifting her head so that her mouth was only inches from his. "I love your freckles." He kissed the tip of her nose. "I adore your mouth." He ran the tip of his tongue over her lips, then kissed her in earnest.

This time Andy allowed the kiss to linger. She was losing the desire to prolong the situation. It would be so much easier to relax and let it happen. But she had determined to keep the reins in her hands. She pushed against his chest. "Slow down. We'll get where you want to go, all in good time."

He leaned back against the couch, his dark gaze fixed on her mouth. "Where we both want to go," he challenged.

"Yes." She smiled and shook back her hair. Leisurely, she loosed the final buttons of his shirt, tugging the tail from his belt to find the last two. She pushed the shirt open and planted a light kiss on his chest, another on his collarbone, another in the indentation at the base of his throat. His breathing had become noticeably faster, and she smiled with satisfaction.

She straightened and walked the fingers of one hand down his chest slowly until she touched his belt buckle. He sucked in his breath, and she tilted her head to gaze at him. With a teasing look, she withdrew her hand. "Shoes first." She knelt on the floor to remove his shoes and socks, then returned to the couch to deal with the belt buckle. "There seems to be a trick to this thing."

"Let me."

She eased his hand back. "No, I'll do it."

Joe's brain clouded. Her scent floated around him. Her clever fingers loosed his belt buckle, then with maddening slowness dealt with buttons and zipper. Groaning, Joe closed his eyes. He was trying to let her lead—she obviously wanted that—but all he could think was now, he had to have her now. He heard her soft sigh, and then her hands left him and he felt the shifting of her weight on the couch. He opened his eyes as she rose. Unable to restrain himself, he grabbed for her, but she evaded him.

She stood in the center of the room and slid the caftan off her shoulders, then down to expose her bare breasts, past her waist, over her hips, and onto the floor. For a long moment, she stood there in nothing but panties, like the fantasy lover in his most erotic dreams. Then she stepped away from the caftan and removed the wisp of white silk. Naked now, she rested her hands on her hips and smiled at him.

As Joe's last thread of control snapped, he stood up, peeled off his trousers and briefs, strode to her and yanked her against him. "No more, Andy," he groaned. "I can't take any more." His mouth crushed hers, and he dragged her back to the couch.

His hands seared her skin, moving everywhere with a frantic restlessness. His mouth burned her throat, her breasts, her stomach, returning again and again to devour her mouth.

Her taste filled him, but he couldn't get enough. Never enough. His hands roamed her body with a desperate urgency to feel more and more. She murmured his name and moved beneath him, and it drove him to the edge. No more waiting. The thought seared through his dazed mind like a red-hot flame. No more.

Sliding his hands beneath her, he cupped her hips and lifted her. He took her without finesse, mindlessly, driving her, driving himself. His mouth crushed hers, and he swallowed her taste, and he couldn't think. He could only need. He raced to fill that need, faster and faster, until he was plunged into a vortex of lights and colors, and it felt as though his very soul were being ripped from him.

When he was conscious again, his full weight was sprawled atop her. He felt too spent to move. He remembered few of the details of the past few minutes, only the massive, driving need and the rending release. What had happened to him? Had this woman bewitched him?

Andy. He had given no thought to Andy during the past few minutes. He had known only that she, and only she, could assuage his need.

Dear God, what kind of animal had he become? Had he hurt her?

He lifted his head to look down at her. She gazed at him with heavy-lidded eyes. Even in the dim room, he recognized the flush of lovemaking on her skin—and the swollen mouth. He had hurt her!

"Andy, I bruised you. I'm so sorry."

Sighing, she ran her hands over his back. "Don't be. I'm not."

He buried his face in her hair and drew in deep, steadying breaths. "I never meant to hurt you."

She turned her head and kissed his brow. "You didn't hurt me. I taunted you. I wanted to make you lose control." She smiled languidly, her breath warm on his face. "My goodness, did I ever get what I asked for."

He lifted his head and nibbled at her lips. "You're the most incredible woman I've ever known."

She sighed happily as his mouth settled on hers. After a moment, she murmured, "I really don't care to be compared to the other women you've known, Joe. I want to be the only woman in your head."

Growling, he nuzzled her throat and the curve of her shoulder. Unbelievably, he felt his body stirring with fresh arousal. He lifted his head to feast on her mouth, taking the kiss deep.

She wrapped her arms around him, knowing that he wanted her again and wanting him in return. Already feeling her blood heating, her limbs loosening, she whispered, "My bed would be more comfortable."

It was in that moment that Joe knew he was in love with her. This was how it felt, then. He wondered when it had happened. He wondered how she would feel about it if she knew. He wondered—but, no, tonight he would wonder about nothing. Tonight he would only feel.

He rose and carried her to the bedroom.

Joe left Andy after midnight, saying that it wouldn't do for the boys to find him there the next morning. They liked and trusted him, he said, and he didn't want to upset the rapport that was developing between them.

After the overwhelming explosion of passion on the couch, Andy and Joe had made tender, lazy love in her bed with the moonlight silvering their bodies. The silence was punctuated by sighs of satisfaction and murmurs of delight. "Don't get up," he told her as he left the bed reluctantly. He dressed and came back to the bedroom to bend over her for a final, lingering kiss.

She touched his face gently. "I'll dream of you."

"Ah, Andy," he said, "I need you, honey." He paused to smooth her tangled hair back from her face. The depths of his feelings for her were still too new for him to give them the substance of words. He knew that Andy was vulnerable to him, but that didn't mean she was in love with him, or that she could necessarily tell the difference at this point. Love was too rare and precious a commodity to take chances with. He would wait until he felt more sure of his ground. He kissed her forehead and whispered again, "I need you, Andy, and not just in bed."

After he was gone, Andy lay on her stomach, her chin resting on her folded arms. Beyond the bedroom windows, the light of a full moon exposed shrubs, trees and corners of the yard that were usually no more than shadowy patches at night. Her emotions had been like that, she mused, blanketed, concealed, until Joe had come into her life. Now the once-hidden landscape of her woman's needs had been brought into sharp focus. When Joe had made love to her, she'd known for the first time what it was to be buffeted by wild storms of passion over which she had no control. And she'd known what it felt like to be so desperately, selfishly in love that she could be jealous of her own children.

These feelings frightened her. At thirty-five, she had never expected to fall so deeply, so helplessly. She had viewed her future as set, centered on her children and her work, with perhaps an occasional friendship with a man to relieve the monotony. When the boys are grown, she had thought, perhaps I'll marry again. She had imagined a sweet, comfortable companion to ease her loneliness when the boys left home. Not someone like Joe, who made her feel anything but comfortable. Never had she imagined anyone like Joe.

It appeared that the best-laid plans of women were no more protected from disruption than those of mice and men. As she finally drifted into sleep, she saw one thing clearly. It wasn't possible to go back. All she could do now was go forward and see what happened.

During the next couple of weeks, Joe frequently spent time with Andy and the boys. Never once did it occur to Andy to wonder what Harley's reaction to a new man in her life might be. If it had occurred to her, she wouldn't have thought that Harley would react strongly, either positively or negatively. One evening in early August, she learned how wrong she could be.

Brad answered Harley's phone call, and things started going downhill immediately. When Harley mentioned coming to Neptune for a visit and wanted to know what weekend would be good, Brad didn't react with the usual enthusiasm. Harley demanded to know what was wrong. He pressed Brad for an answer until Brad blurted out, "I guess I don't think you'll really come to see us, Dad. You don't keep your promises. You said you'd take us camping last month, but you didn't show up. You didn't even call to let us know you weren't coming. Tony was so mad he ran away from home."

Listening to Brad's end of the conversation, Andy could imagine Harley trying to justify himself. But Brad wasn't buying it. At one point, Brad shrugged and said, "No, he's all right. We found him, and we got to go camping, after all. Joe and Mom took us. We had a great time."

Oh, Lord, Andy thought, as she finished putting the dinner dishes in the washer. Now she would get the third degree when she spoke to her ex-husband. Then Tony came into the kitchen, and Brad seemed relieved to see him. "Tony's here now, Dad. I'll let you talk to him."

Tony took the phone and, barely pausing to say hello, began to tell his father about going fishing with Joe that previous week. "You should've seen the catfish I caught, Dad! He was a giant! Joe said he was a granddaddy. Mom cooked our catch in the backyard, and Grandpa came over, and we really pigged out." At that point, Harley must have asked if Tony was enjoying the use of his backpack, for Tony said, "The one Mom got me for my birthday? Oh, sure. I love it. I use it all the time." Tony glanced over at Andy, who was cleaning the cabinet top with a damp cloth. "Mom, he wants to talk to you."

Andy squared her shoulders and took the receiver from Tony. Brad and Tony left the kitchen as she said, "Hello, Harley. How are you?"

"I'm damned confused!" Harley said petulantly.

"Oh?"

"What garbage have you been feeding my sons about me?"

"I've never tried to turn Brad and Tony against you, Harley," Andy said, determined to remain calm. "You know I wouldn't do that."

"Then what's the idea of telling Tony you bought that backpack? The last time we talked, you said you put my name on it."

"I did." Andy sighed and went on reluctantly. "Harley, we were having some problems with Tony. I heard Brad tell you he ran away after you didn't show up for the camping trip."

"Oh, hell, yes. It's all my fault!"

"I didn't say that. I'm not a perfect parent, either. But when Tony ran away, I realized I was going to have to be more honest with the boys. We talked about a lot of things, and I told Tony the truth about the backpack."

"What did you tell them about me?" Harley demanded.

"Only the truth as I see it. I said that you love them and that you wouldn't deliberately lie to them, but that you have your faults, like everybody else."

"All of which faults you no doubt pointed out to them!"

"It wasn't like that, Harley," Andy said in exasperation. "I've simply decided not to make excuses for you anymore. From now on you'll have to do your own explaining to Brad and Tony."

"Damn it, Andy, you're taking advantage of the fact that you're with them all the time, and I'm here where I don't see them very often."

"Whose fault is that?"

He quickly switched the subject. "Who the hell is Joe?"

Andy had known the question was coming, and she said casually, "Oh, just a man who moved here to work at the new automobile plant."

"Are you sleeping with him?"

Andy gripped the telephone and forced herself to say calmly, "That's none of your business, Harley. I don't ask you about your women. I will say that I've been seeing quite a lot of Joe."

"Well, hell, it's my business when a stranger starts worming his way between me and my kids. Sounds to me like the boys are seeing as much of this Joe dude as you are. Has he moved in with you?"

"No. Not that it would be any of your business if he had."

"It damn well is my business! I won't stand for another man playing dad to my kids. You get that, Andy?"

Andy counted to ten before replying. "Brad and Tony know who their father is."

"Yeah, well, I'm going to make sure they don't forget. I've got some time off this month. I want Brad and Tony to fly down here for two weeks. I'll send the plane tickets."

Andy chose her words carefully. "I think I'll wait until I get the tickets to mention this to them."

"Are you calling me a liar?"

Andy bit her tongue to keep from replying in the affirmative.

"Our divorce settlement gave me liberal visiting rights," Harley went on furiously. "I don't have to have your permission to see my sons!"

"I know what our agreement was," Andy said coolly. "I'll live up to my end when you live up to yours."

"What the hell are you talking about?"

"You're eight months behind in the support payments, and we could use the money. The boys have outgrown everything this summer. They're going to need new school clothes. When you send the plane tickets, include a check for the back payments. If I don't get some money soon, Harley, I'll have to see an attorney."

There was a shocked silence on the other end of the line. Then Harley thundered, "You're mighty sassy since you've got another man in your bed! Well, you'll get the damned support money, Andy. I don't have it, but I'll get it somehow. And I'll send the tickets for Brad and Tony."

"Fine."

"Tell your new stud to stay away from my sons!" Harley banged down the phone before Andy could reply.

As Andy replaced the receiver, she noticed that her hand was shaking. Harley was angrier than she could ever remember him being. She had heard alarm in his voice, too. Perhaps he had never expected Andy to become involved with another man, any more than she had. Harley had neglected his sons and now he was imagining an interloper moving in and winning Brad's and Tony's loyalty. Apparently he was determined to recover lost ground.

He'll simmer down, Andy told herself as she turned away from the phone. He probably wouldn't even send the plane tickets. But if he did, it would be good for the boys to spend two weeks in Florida with their father. She had always expected them to visit their father occasionally. It was nothing to worry about.

Nevertheless, Andy was uneasy.

Chapter Thirteen

Ten days later, on a Saturday afternoon, Andy and Joe drove the boys to Omaha, where they would board a plane for Florida. To Andy's surprise, Harley had sent the plane tickets with a check for almost half of the overdue support money. There had also been a curt note promising the rest before the end of the month.

Having never expected Harley to send for the boys, Andy found she was having mixed feelings about letting them go. Not that she could very well stop them. The judge had granted Harley generous visitation rights, though Harley had failed to take advantage of that before. His request for a two-week visit was surprising but reasonable, Andy told herself. Had Harley been another kind of father, he might have had the boys with him most of the summer, and she wouldn't have objected strenuously. Yet she couldn't shake the feeling of unease that had been with her since Harley's angry telephone conversation.

He had called again, a few days later, to confirm his plans with the boys, but he hadn't asked to speak to Andy. That, too, seemed somehow ominous. It indicated he was still angry with her, although Harley usually got over his bursts of temper quickly.

He was up to something. Andy pushed the thought aside the instant it was formed. She was being ridiculous, an overanxious mother.

They checked the bags and reached the boarding gate fifteen minutes before the flight was scheduled to leave.

Andy smoothed Tony's shirt collar. "Now, don't forget. In case your father is delayed, you're to wait for him at the gate where you get off. Don't go to the baggage area until he gets there."

"How can we forget, Mom?" Tony asked. "You've told us about ten times."

Andy glanced at Joe over Tony's head, and Joe cocked an eyebrow as though to say, He's right, Andy. She turned to Brad. "You'll call me in a couple of days?"

"Sure, Mom."

"Dad's going to take us to Disney World," Tony informed Joe. "Epcot Center, too. Gosh, I can't wait!"

"You guys are making me envious," Joe said, grinning. "While you're traipsing all over Florida, enjoying yourselves, you might give a thought or two to your Mom and me back home, with our noses to the grindstone."

"Boo hoo," Brad groaned and punched Joe's arm playfully. He turned to Andy. "We're really gonna miss you, Mom. I wish you were coming with us."

Hugging him, Andy swallowed the lump that had lodged in her throat. "We'll talk on the phone every couple of days. Besides, you're going to be so busy you won't have time to miss me."

"Joe, will you come with Mom to meet us when we get back?" Tony asked.

"You bet."

A voice came over the loudspeaker, announcing the boarding of the Florida flight. Amid a flurry of back patting, hugging and kissing, Joe and Andy told the boys goodbye. They watched Brad and Tony dash excitedly to the boarding tunnel and disappear from sight.

Joe put an arm around Andy. "Come on, let's take a look around town and find some place to have dinner."

With a final look over her shoulder, Andy allowed him to lead her away. "I thought we'd head straight back."

"What's the hurry?" He eyed her askance. "You don't have a date with somebody else tonight, do you?"

That elicited a smile. "What would you do if I said yes?"

"Make sure my car broke down."

She glanced up into the teasing glint in his eyes. "I didn't know you had a devious side."

He held a door open for her to pass through. They walked a few steps and got on an escalator. Joe stood on the step behind her, his hands resting easily on her shoulders. "Every man has a devious side," he observed, "if he thinks he's in danger of losing something important to him."

"Yeah," she murmured gravely, thinking of Harley. "I suppose you're right."

"You're still worried about sending the boys to Florida."

They got off the escalator, left the terminal and walked the short distance to Joe's car. The sun was very low in the western sky as they drove away from the airport.

Joe pulled into a line of traffic and reached for her hand. "Andy, they'll be okay."

"I know, only... Why didn't Harley send round-trip tickets?"

"We talked about this before and decided he probably didn't have enough money when he bought the tickets."

"I hope that's the reason," she said. "I can pay for their return tickets if that's all it is."

"Honey, what else could it be? You don't think he'd skip out with them, do you?"

"A couple of weeks ago, I'd have said no way."

"Andy, his character hasn't undergone a transformation simply because you're seeing another man. Look, the boys got to him when they told him how much time they'd been spending with me. He knows he's been remiss as a father, and he feels guilty. So he decided to go all out to show them a good time that they won't soon forget. You can understand that. After two weeks, he'll be more than ready to put them on the plane for home."

"I suppose," she admitted. "They were so excited about going, and I guess I'm feeling a little unappreciated right now. Silly, isn't it?"

"Yes, it is. Don't make this a contest as to which parent they love more."

"I wouldn't do that to Brad and Tony. I know they love me, and they love their father." She took a long, bracing breath and squeezed his hand, as though to reassure herself that she had something solid to hold on to. "That's as it should be."

"It is, Andy. You'll keep busy, and the two weeks will pass quickly. In the meantime, you might as well concentrate on other things."

"You're right." She pushed the unreasoning anxiety to the back of her mind. "I know you're right." Deliberately, she turned toward him and enclosed his hand in both of hers. "I'll concentrate on other things. Did you have anything particular in mind?" she murmured as she leaned over to place a light kiss on his ear.

"Actually, I did. Let's stay in a hotel tonight and go home tomorrow."

Making an effort, Andy shook off the lingering tendrils of uneasiness. "You didn't think of that just now, did you?"

Joe grinned at her expression. "I've been pondering it for a while. I didn't want to mention it until we were alone."

"Well, we have nobody to answer to for a couple of weeks except ourselves. I'd have to call Pop, of course, so he won't worry."

Freeing his hand from hers, he reached out and pulled her head down to rest on his shoulder. He was glad to feel the tension easing out of her. "How will Bo feel about our staying overnight?"

"He would never say." With a smile, Andy settled comfortably against him. "There are some things about which he won't offer unsolicited opinions. I doubt that he'll be shocked, though."

"No, not Bo." He gave her a quick kiss on the nose. "I don't think there's much about human nature that would shock him."

"Keep your eyes on the road," she instructed, then glanced at her watch. "It's after six, and I had an early lunch. When do we eat?"

"We'll find a hotel first, and you can call your father. Then you can concentrate on me for the rest of the evening."

"That sounds like fun," Andy said with a laugh. "While I'm doing that, you can concentrate on me."

"Exactly what I had in mind," Joe told her as he caught sight of a large new hotel and turned off the freeway.

Mellowed by the champagne they'd drunk and anticipating finally having Andy alone, Joe opened the door of their hotel room. Dinner had relaxed her, slowly releasing her from thoughts of the boys and whatever trouble she imagined Harley might be concocting. As for Joe, he sensed a new element in their relationship tonight, an unhurried, comfortable intimacy, free—at least for now—of problems and distractions. Now they were just a man and a woman who wanted very much to be together.

"I'm going to loll in the Jacuzzi," Andy stated, walking into the room and kicking off her shoes. She headed for the bathroom. "There's plenty of room for two," she tossed casually over her shoulder.

Andy turned on the jets, undressed and lowered herself slowly into the warm, swirling water. Sighing, she slid down until the water reached her shoulders. She lifted her hair off her neck and tipped her head back to rest on the Jacuzzi's smoothly rounded rim. Water gushed from a jet behind her to massage her hips and thighs. It felt utterly wonderful, utterly relaxing. She had risen at dawn to help the boys pack. Then there had been the long drive to Omaha, and the stress on her nervous system of seeing them off and dealing with her anxiety over Harley's continuing ill feelings. She was, she realized, very weary. A little moan of pure contentment escaped her, and her eyes drifted closed.

Perhaps she dozed, she couldn't be sure. In a half-dreaming state, she heard the rustle of clothes being removed and dropped to the tile floor. Then there was a soft, splashing sound as Joe joined her in the tub.

She didn't stir as he sank into the water and moved toward her. She sat with her head back, eyes closed, her hair fanning out over the edge of the Jacuzzi. He would have thought she was asleep except for the smile that whispered over her mouth. He had known, all evening, that this night would be touched with magic. It was in the air, in every word and glance they had exchanged. He had only to look at her like this to become instantly aroused, but he fought back his throbbing need.

Reaching for her, he brushed the hair off her forehead with both hands and planted soft kisses along her hairline. Then he kissed her eyelids, and finally, he allowed himself a delectable taste of her mouth. He inhaled the feminine scent that was especially Andy's—clean skin and hair and the light fragrance of her cologne. Her scent seduced him, and for an instant he thought he would get lost in it. He struggled to hold on, and after a long moment he lifted his head. He could see her pulse throbbing madly in the hollow at the base of her throat.

She dragged her eyelids open; the effort was almost too much for her. "Joe..." she murmured, her mind dazed by drowsiness and the warm, swirling water.

Her shuddering, indrawn breath seemed to mesh with his own heartbeat. Gazing at him, she touched his face wonderingly. He wanted to crush her to him, to drown in her sweetness. But he restrained himself. Go with the magic, he told himself. I adore you, Andy.

"I must have been asleep," she murmured. "This could be a dream." Her fingers caressed his cheek. "A lovely dream..." She watched his pupils darken with desire, and suddenly she plunged her fingers into his hair and pulled his mouth to hers. If I'm dreaming, let me never wake up, was all she could think. Never.

He groaned deep in his throat as his hands flowed over her body beneath the warm water—the breasts that fitted perfectly in his cupped hands, the incredibly slender waist, the sleek thighs, the taut stomach, the soft mound of her womanhood. His blood raced, thick and hot. Passion was a whirlpool, like the water swirling all around them, sucking him down. He battled the impulse to take her wordlessly, to let himself go and give in to the mindlessness. No, this was a magic night, the night he had been waiting for, he told himself. No more waiting now. No more caution. No more self-protection. He was going to lay bare his heart.

Her mouth on his had become seeking, hungry. He pulled back from the precipice, lifted his head to look at her. Her face was rosy and moist, her heavy-lidded eyes a deep, deep blue, her warm breath whispering between softly parted lips. Emotions flooded him as he studied her—a painfully sharp hunger tempered by an aching tenderness. He knew that he wanted to see her like this every night, to wake each morning to find her beside him. He knew, too, that life without her would be a barren desert. Bending, he brushed his lips over hers.

"Andy," he murmured as she sighed and skimmed her palms down his back. Whispering her name again, he traced kisses over her face, nibbling lightly at her lips until she caught his head in her hands to press her mouth to his. "Andy," he said against her lips. "I love you."

She caught her breath. Her eyes flew open, and she stared at him. "What did you say?"

"I'm in love with you," he said gravely. Then he clasped her head, and his mouth plundered hers. With a ragged, oxygen-starved breath, he groaned, "Oh, God, I love you so much."

With a gasp and a smile as brilliant as a sunrise, she stroked her hands over his smooth, muscled flesh and blazed a trail of wet, open-mouthed kisses along his neck and shoulder.

He clasped her chin between his fingers and lifted her head. He looked at her through a haze of adoration and need and thought his laboring heart would explode in his chest. "Andy, do you love me?"

She gave him another blinding smile. "Madly. I thought you knew."

With a groan thick with gratitude and desire, he covered her mouth with his. He moved above her, wet skin sliding over wet skin, and entered her slowly, smoothly. Around them steam rose from the lapping, swirling water. Beneath the liquid surface, continuous gushing streams of water from the Jacuzzi's jets flowed over their slick bodies.

Swept into the whirlpool with him, Andy lost herself in a rapturous spiral. Clinging to him, she matched the slow, erotic tempo of his lovemaking until the world was distilled to nothing but Joe's mouth ravishing hers and his hard, wet body sliding against her, pushing her closer and closer to the eddying descent. Then, with little warning, they reached the center of passion's whirlpool and plunged in. There was a blinding flash of heat and sensation followed by ripples of release that went on and on.

Buffeted by a physical response that was intensified by violent emotions, Andy felt as though she were being splintered into a million fragments. Drained and dazed in the aftermath, she finally felt herself slowly coalescing again. Awareness moved outside of her, and she became conscious of Joe's body wound around hers, of his labored breathing as he rested his cheek against hers. With leaden arms, she held him and closed her eyes against the hot stinging that she knew would be a deluge if she allowed it to become tears.

Joe was too spent to move. His limbs quivered with the relaxation of tension, and he dragged air into his lungs in deep gulps. Slowly, coherence returned. She loved him. It was no fantasy—she had really said it. In a few minutes of time, his whole world had been altered. He was finished with looking over his shoulder at the past. For the first time, he felt as though he had really buried his dead. Andy was his future now. There was nothing they couldn't face together.

Like a man tossed ashore by a passing hurricane, he was dazed and staggered by his good fortune. He lifted his head, which still felt too heavy for his neck to support, and looked down at her. Her lashes were dark and wet against the rosy flush of her cheeks. Her hair was damp and tangled, her breath still coming a little too quickly. She was incredibly beautiful to him.

"Andy, I adore you."

Without opening her eyes she sighed softly and let her hand trail over his back. She was only now beginning to comprehend what had passed between them. She didn't want to move too quickly and destroy the wonder that was still washing through her. Smiling, she opened her eyes. "I didn't dream it, then. I was afraid I had. I didn't see how you could love me as much as I love you. There's so much, apart from ourselves, to deal with."

She saw gratitude flood into his eyes. He feathered kisses over her face. "If you're worried about the boys, don't. I've always known how important they are to you. The maternal side of you is part of your charm, sweetheart. I wouldn't have it any other way."

No other way? What exactly did he mean? But Andy was too tired to deal with such questions tonight. Joe had said he loved her. She would let that be enough for now. "Let's go to bed," she murmured. "I feel as though I could sleep for twelve hours straight."

"Yeah. Me, too."

They climbed out of the Jacuzzi, dried themselves and fell into bed. "Honey," he murmured against her hair, "you make me very happy. Thank you."

Already half-asleep, Andy sighed, "You're welcome, my darling."

Turning on his side, he pulled her back against him, spoon fashion. They were both asleep within seconds.

Once back in Neptune, Andy spent every evening with Joe. They laughed together, relaxed together, talked for hours, and made love. Joe spoke frequently of things they would do with the boys when Brad and Tony came home. He wanted them to get used to having him around, he said. He didn't want them to feel any jealousy or resentment toward him when they realized he and Andy had fallen in love.

Andy vacillated between being troubled by Joe's frequent mention of the children and being grateful that he was obviously so fond of them. But she had other things on her mind, as well.

When the boys didn't phone two days after their arrival, as promised, Andy tried to call them. There was no answer at Harley's apartment in Gainesville. By the end of the fourth day, she was gripped by anxiety. Joe was working late at the office, although he had promised to come by if he finished before ten. Otherwise, he would telephone to say good-night.

Alone, Andy wandered through the house, going to the phone every half hour to dial the Gainesville number. When her telephone, which had been silent all evening, rang at nine-thirty, she nearly jumped out of her skin. She jerked the receiver off the hook in the kitchen.

"Hello?"

"Mom, it's Brad."

Andy's knees suddenly gave way, and she sank into a chair. "Oh, thank goodness! Brad, I've been trying to reach you since night before last. You promised you'd call."

"I'm sorry, Mom. I meant to, but we've been too busy. We've been getting back to the hotel real late, and Dad said we'd wake you if we called."

Damn you, Harley, Andy fumed silently. "I don't care how late it is. I want to hear from you regularly."

"Well, okay. I just thought—I mean, Dad said..."

"It's all right, Brad. Where are you calling from?"

"Orlando. We're staying in this really neat hotel. There's a big room with video games and pool tables and everything."

"That's nice. Is everything all right?"

"Sure." He sounded puzzled by her question. "Mom, Dad will be back in a minute and we're going down to play pool. Tony wants to talk to you now."

"Mom?"

"Hi, Tony. I miss you, honey."

"Mom, we're having the most fun! We've been to Disney World twice—and Epcot and Sea World!"

"That sounds wonderful, Tony. I'm glad you're having a good time."

"Dad said he wishes we lived near him so we could do stuff together all the time."

"Oh?" Andy's anxiety was back in full force. "Well, that would be nice," she said judiciously. "Is there any chance your father might move closer to us?"

"I don't know. He sure does like Florida. Golly, who wouldn't! There are so many fun things to do here. As soon as we finish in Orlando, we're going to Key West and see the ocean and swim and go sailing."

"When?"

"I'm not sure."

"But you'll be going to Key West next?"

"I guess so. Mom, Dad's here. I have to go now."

"Tony," Andy said urgently, "you and Brad call me again before Sunday. Promise."

"Okay, Mom. Listen, they're going out the door. I gotta go. Bye."

Beset by a flood of misgivings, Andy hung up. Too agitated to stay put any longer, she went next door. Looking through the open screen door, she saw Bo seated on the couch, a TV tray in front of him. Papers were strewn over the tray. Andy knocked. "Pop."

He gestured without looking up. "Come on in."

She perched on the arm of the couch. "Contest entries?"

He nodded and chewed the eraser end of his pencil. "It's hard to explain in just twenty-five words why you should win a Florida vacation."

"You need Brad's and Tony's input," Andy said morosely. "I just talked to them on the phone. They didn't call sooner because they don't get back to the hotel until late at night. Harley told them they'd wake me if they called. Meanwhile, I've been tearing my hair out, wondering why I haven't heard from them."

Bo frowned and tossed his pencil down. "Harley told them not to call?"

"Yeah. What a guy, huh?"

"That's downright mean. What's come over Harley?"

"He's trying to spite me."

Bo's bushy brows shot up. "Why?"

"Oh, Pop, it's a long story. The short version is that he found out I've been seeing a lot of Joe, and that the boys have, too, and he—well, he sort of panicked, I think. He told me he wouldn't stand for another man playing father to his kids. Apparently, he's been entertaining them to the hilt since they got off the plane in Florida. Just now, on the phone, Tony told me Harley's been making noises about what a shame it is the boys live so far away because he wants to spend more time with them."

"All of a sudden, he's decided to make up for the past two years?"

"Evidently. I'm scared, Pop. I have this uneasy feeling Harley's got something up his sleeve."

"Like what?"

"I wish I knew."

"Andy, I think you're working yourself up needlessly. Sure, it's hard to compete with this—this emotional blackmail of Harley's, but even Disney World palls if you go there every day. It can't last. The boys will be back at the end of the week, and school will start and things will get back to normal. When everything's said and done, kids remember who's there for them day in and day out, through thick and thin."

"You really think so, Pop?"

"You bet. You do too, if you'll just relax and stop conjuring up things to worry about."

Andy leaned over and kissed his cheek. "Thanks, Pop. I'll try to take your advice." She slid off the couch arm. "I'd better go home now. I'm expecting Joe to call."

Bo cocked his head and eyed her speculatively. "Seeing a lot of that young man, aren't you?"

"Uh-huh." Andy paused at the door. "Joe's very special, Pop."

"You won't get any arguments from me. I like the man."

Everybody liked Joe, it seemed. Everybody but Harley, Andy reflected as she walked back home. Bo's reassurances had been momentarily uplifting, but that didn't last. Nor did Joe's phone call at ten that night pull her completely out of her depression. He was still at the office, trying to finish a proposed marketing campaign plan, and would probably be there for another hour. He wouldn't be coming by.

When she told him about her conversation with the boys, he advised her to forget it. "Let's go somewhere for the weekend," he suggested. "It'll be our last chance to get away together before Brad and Tony get back."

"I can't. I want to be here in case they call."

Joe didn't press her. "Okay, we'll hang out at your house all weekend. I'll do the cooking."

"You don't have to do that."

"Andy, let me spoil you a little. I'm crazy about you, woman. You and your kids and your old man. I love you so much I'm in love with everybody who's related to you."

"Oh, Joe..."

"Are you crying?"

Andy swallowed hard. "Of course not. Will you come over tomorrow evening?"

"Try to keep me away."

She grinned. "Why should I do that?"

"Ah, Andy... I'd better get back to work."

"Good night, Joe."

Andy wandered through the house, turning out lights. *I'm in love with everybody who's related to you.* Joe's words echoed through her mind as she got ready for bed. It had been nearly a week since he'd first told her he loved her, but she was still finding it difficult to believe unreservedly.

What did she expect of the man? she wondered as she crawled between cool sheets.

She wanted to be loved for herself alone. Was that really so much to ask?

Chapter Fourteen

Joe's presence made the weekend easier for Andy to get through, even though she didn't hear from the boys. She knew that somehow Harley was preventing their calling, and that made her furiously angry. But when she was with Joe, he helped her forget her anger, sometimes for hours at a time.

"He's angling to get your goat," Joe told her Sunday evening. "Don't let him do it."

"I'm trying," Andy replied. But she had never been in a war of nerves with Harley before. He'd always been easygoing, willing to let her take responsibility for the boys. She'd never seen this vengeful side of him, but then she had never crossed him when they were married. She'd certainly never looked at another man. She had never given Harley any reason to want to hurt her. Even when she asked him for a divorce, she had managed to salve his ego by making it sound as though she blamed herself for the split.

She didn't know how to begin trying to find Harley and the boys by telephone. She simply had to wait for them to make contact. When the boys did call, she told herself, she would insist on talking to Harley. She would pin him down as to the day, hour and minute when he meant to put the boys on a plane for home.

The phone call came Tuesday evening. They'd just returned to Gainesville from Key West where they'd sailed, snorkeled and taken scuba diving lessons, Tony said in the same breath with hello. He sounded as excited as ever; if anything, he seemed even more wound up and tense.

"Maybe you can just rest for a few days," Andy said, "now that you're back at your father's place. You must all be exhausted."

"Yeah," Tony agreed, "Dad's getting kinda cranky. He called Donna, and she's coming over with pizza."

Who was Donna? Andy wondered, but refrained from asking. Must be Harley's latest love interest. She also refrained from scolding Tony for not having called sooner. She knew it wasn't his fault. "When are you coming home?" Andy asked.

"Uh—I'm not sure," Tony said vaguely. "Dad wants to talk to you now, Mom. Here he is."

"Harley," Andy exploded as soon as she heard his voice, "what the hell is going on with you? The boys were supposed to call me three days ago!"

"Just a minute," Harley said and although he put his hand over the phone, she could still hear his muffled words. He was sending the boys out of the room. Then he said, "Time got away from us, Andy."

"I don't believe that, Harley. I think you wouldn't let them call!"

"I figured old Joe would keep you from getting lonely." The sarcasm in his voice was blatant now.

"Like old Donna does for you?"

"Huh? Oh. Tony told you about Donna, eh? Well, damn it, Andy, are you the only one who's allowed to get laid?"

"I couldn't care less if you get laid every hour on the hour!" Andy fumed. "All I want to know is when I can expect the boys back home."

"I need to talk to you about that."

An odd shiver skipped up Andy's spine. "So talk."

"I've been discussing with Brad and Tony the possibility of them staying here with me longer than we originally planned."

"You've what!" Andy sputtered. She paused for a long moment, forcing herself to calm down. In a more reasonable tone, she said, "You shouldn't have done that, Harley. School starts in less than three weeks. They have to be here to enroll and get school supplies and new clothes. They can't possibly stay beyond this weekend."

"I was thinking they could go to school here."

Andy was stunned into momentary speechlessness. She had been waiting for ten days for Harley to drop the other shoe, and he finally had. This was what he'd had up his sleeve all along. This was why he'd been knocking himself out to show the boys a good time. All of it had been to make Brad and Tony want to stay with him permanently. It was bribery, pure and simple.

"No." She cut the words off sharply, giving it the sound of finality.

"Andy, I want to discuss this like two adults. I'm their father, for God's sake."

"And I have custody. You agreed to that without any argument."

"People can change their minds," he said ominously, "and custody agreements can be changed, too—if you insist on forcing the issue. I think I could get joint custody, at least."

"You're damned right I'll force the issue! Besides, I can't believe Brad and Tony want to move to Gainesville permanently."

"Don't be too sure of that."

"You've talked to them about it?"

"Some."

The snake! Oh, God…why was Harley doing this? A sharp pain suddenly cramped Andy's hand, making her aware of how hard she was clutching the phone receiver. Her stomach churned, and tears of frustration were very close to the surface. She took a deep breath. "You do what you have to do, Harley. In the meantime, I have custody, and I want those boys back here next weekend."

"I figured you'd be unreasonable." He sounded amazingly unperturbed. Was it possible that the boys actually did want to stay with their father permanently? Could he have won them over so completely in ten days? She remembered how charming Harley could be when he wanted something, and she trembled with the beginning of panic. "This is all academic, anyway," Harley was saying.

Andy forced down hysteria in an effort to understand his meaning. "Academic? What does that mean?"

"Brad will be thirteen next month, or had you forgotten?"

"I'm not in the habit of forgetting my son's birthdays," Andy shot back, unable to resist the jibe. "But what does that have to do with anything?"

Harley paused, as though for effect, then said calmly, "At thirteen, a kid can decide for himself which parent he wants to live with. Now, Tony won't be thirteen for awhile, but I figured you wouldn't want to separate them."

Andy supposed there was a law like that. She seemed to remember having heard something about judges allowing children in their teens to choose their custodial parent. She'd never given it any thought because it hadn't occurred to her that anything like this would ever come up between her and Harley. How was she supposed to deal with this on the telephone? Impossible. As impossible as giving Harley permission to keep the boys. Would he actually take her to court—take them all to court? "Let me talk to Brad."

"No can do. I sent them out for ice cream."

"You're a—a sneak and a jerk, Harley. We have nothing more to discuss. If you don't have the money to send them back next weekend, I can arrange for their plane tickets."

"I'll buy the tickets," he said irritably, "when I'm ready. You're wrong about the other thing, too. We have plenty to discuss. When you can be reasonable, give me a call.''

Andy opened her mouth and heard the dial tone. Harley had hung up on her! Instantly, she dialed Harley's number. But before the connection was made, she slammed the receiver down. She was too upset to talk to him now. She'd only make matters worse.

Numb and nauseated, Andy sat on the couch. Her fingers gripping the couch arm were cold and nerveless. She knew she had to pull herself together so that she could think. She felt alone and deserted, but if she tried to talk to her father or Joe now, she would come apart. She sat as still as a rock and waited for the sick feeling to pass.

Harley couldn't do this, could he? She would get a lawyer. She'd sue the pants off him. She'd... But what would going to court do to the boys? They'd be in the middle, between fighting parents. It could scar them for life.

Ironically, she thought of how she'd resented Harley's failure to spend any time with the boys since the divorce. She hadn't known when she was well-off. Now she realized how much easier it had been on her when Harley didn't want to assume any responsibility.

But he was only doing this because of Joe. He was acting impulsively, out of anger and fear of being displaced in his sons' affections. Given more time, he'd see it wasn't all fun and games, having the full-time responsibility for two adolescent boys, and he'd change his mind. Harley had never had any staying power. When things got tough, he ducked out. So why couldn't she stop shaking with fear?

If it came to a court battle, could she put the boys through that? What if Brad actually had decided he wanted to live with Harley? Wouldn't he resent her if she forced him to remain with her? If Brad stayed with Harley, Tony might want to stay, too. If that happened, she didn't think she could make Tony live with her against his will. Besides, brothers should grow up together.

Maybe Harley would back off if she stopped seeing Joe. The thought was a deeper pain in a morass of anguish. Andy had never felt more lost in her life than she did at that moment. Joe. Dear God, she needed Joe. How could she give up the man she loved more than her own life? She closed her eyes as the pain rose and ebbed.

She couldn't give Joe up, and she couldn't give up her children. Perhaps the decision would be taken from her hands, she reflected, as fresh fear crawled through her. If she lost the boys, Joe might no longer want her. She had never known how much of his need for her was mixed up with his need for a family.

She thought of the intimacy that had grown between them over the summer. Joe's smile. His lovemaking. The way he could make her feel completely a woman, as she'd never felt before in her life. And his patience and rapport with the boys. How often he had mentioned them during the past several days. She knew that he was looking forward to their return; he'd said as much.

Love. How much did Joe love her? Not Bo's daughter or Brad and Tony's mother, but just Andy.

Ultimately, she would have to know. Soon. With a sigh, Andy stared at her wristwatch. Joe would be there in thirty minutes to take her to dinner. She could say she was too ill to go out, but then she'd be alone with her terrifying thoughts. It would be better to go. Perhaps before the evening was over she would know what to do about Harley. She had to do something.

She looked around the living room. It was clean and neat. No half-finished models or baseball cards or the remains of a cookie crunched beneath a boy's heedless foot. No dirty underwear or tennis shoes lying about. And such quiet was almost unnerving. The neatness and silence were pleasant as an occasional reprieve, but not as a way of life.

Andy took a deep breath and rose from the couch. Squaring her shoulders, she walked to the bedroom to change for dinner.

When Andy answered Joe's knock, he handed her two dozen long-stemmed yellow roses. She held them to her breast and had to blink to keep back tears. Her emotions were dangerously near the surface. To hide her face from Joe while she composed herself, she buried it in the roses.

"They're so beautiful," she murmured. Feeling steadier, she lifted her face for his kiss. "Thank you, Joe. Is this a special occasion?"

His eyes were brimming with warmth. "Any time I'm with you, it's a special occasion."

That wasn't really an answer, Andy thought, as she found a vase and put the roses in water. She set the roses on the coffee table.

She looks tired, Joe thought. As if she hadn't slept well in days. "Andy, are you all right?"

"It's been a trying afternoon. I'll tell you about it later." She reached for his hand. "Shall we go?" She wasn't sure she would be able to eat, but she desperately wanted to get out of that neat, silent house for a few hours.

Joe shot her a look. "Not yet. What's wrong, honey?"

She shut her eyes at that, thinking how well he sensed her moods. "It's...nothing." She felt suddenly awkward, standing there, purse in hand, with Joe blocking the door. Tossing her purse on the couch, she walked to a window and gazed out, seeing nothing.

"Andy, you asked me if tonight was a special occasion," Joe said, moving restlessly about the room. "Well, I meant it to be. I was going to wait until later—after dinner. Now, I don't think I'll wait."

Struggling to free herself from her gloom, Andy turned around. "I'm sorry, Joe. I wasn't listening. What did you say?"

He gave a quick, harsh laugh. "Great. I'm baring my soul for you, and you aren't listening."

Distressed by his tone and the hurt in his eyes, Andy took a step toward him. "I'm...sorry," she said helplessly.

"Don't keep saying that. The last thing I want from you is sympathy." He raked a hand through his hair, then stuffed both hands into his trousers pockets, as though regretting the tension-betraying gesture.

Nonplussed, Andy suggested, "Perhaps we should go to dinner now."

"No."

Her chin jerked up at the determination in the word. "All right." She lifted her shoulders. "I'm not hungry, anyway. We can stay here. I can rustle up something for you."

"Andy, will you shut up for a minute?"

She looked at him in astonishment.

His eyes held hers for a long moment. "I'm trying to ask you to marry me." He watched as her eyes widened, then narrowed so that he could read nothing in them.

"What did you say?"

"I want you to be my wife."

To Andy, the few steps separating them yawned as wide as a canyon. She had imagined him saying those words, had wanted desperately to hear them. But it was no longer a simple matter of saying yes—though it was a struggle to keep the word from slipping out. Joe didn't know what she'd been hit with that day. The irony of it! Shaken, she gripped the back of a chair.

"If you need time to think about it—"

"Don't." She lifted a hand as though to ward off evil.

He came to her then. Bewildered and angered by her reaction, he grabbed her and yanked her against him. For an instant they stared at each other, and then his mouth was on hers, demanding, possessing. She loved him, damn it! He'd make her admit it. She didn't fight him. She merely went limp in his arms. Why wasn't she responding to him? On a wave of fear, he lifted his head. Her eyes were brimming with tears. "God, Andy, tell me what's wrong."

She swallowed hard. "Yes, I'll tell you. Let's sit down." They sat on the couch, side by side, but not touching. Staring at the hands clasped in her lap, Andy said, "I talked to Harley this evening. He wants permission to keep the boys with him. He's been talking to them about starting school in Gainesville. He reminded me that Brad will be thirteen next month, and a judge would probably let him decide where he wants to live."

Tears trickled down her cheeks, unheeded. She took a shaky breath and went on, "Harley threatened to go to court if I force the issue. He must believe Brad would choose to stay with him, or he wouldn't risk going before a judge. I could probably retain custody of Tony, but I'm not sure that would be the best thing for him—to drag this through court and then separate him from Brad, I mean." She choked back a sob. "Oh, Joe, I'm so furious and so scared. Harley hasn't paid any attention to Brad and Tony since the divorce, and now—I never imagined...I just don't know what to do."

He waited while she extracted a tissue from her purse and dried her cheeks. Then he said carefully, "Maybe you should give Harley a chance, honey."

Andy stared at him as she tried to sort out her thoughts. "Give Harley a chance!"

"What I mean is, if Harley really wants to take on the responsibility, maybe you should let the boys decide. Look, sweetheart, I know it would be tough to let them go, and I think they'd be much better off with you. But if you force them to come back here against their will, they'll see Harley as the wronged party, and they'll resent you."

Brows drawn together, she listened to Joe's words. She didn't want to admit that he was right. She said stiffly, "I thought you'd have a fit. I thought..." She gazed at him a moment and then swallowed her pride. "I—I thought you wanted the boys as much as you wanted me."

He shook his head, and his hands lifted to her shoulders. His fingers tightened. "I love those kids, Andy. I'm going to miss them like hell if they stay in Florida. But that has absolutely nothing to do with the way I feel about you. I love you. I want to spend the rest of my life with you."

She swallowed as a wave of hope washed over her. "Even if—if Brad and Tony don't live with us?"

"I'm not asking Brad and Tony to marry me. Andy, you're the only woman I've ever loved as a man should love his wife. Honey, I don't care if you come with no kids or a dozen. It's you I want."

She blinked back fresh tears and met his eyes. "I love you," she whispered, then let out a long, shuddering breath. With it went her doubts.

"Then answer my question. Will you marry me?"

She didn't hesitate. "Yes." She went into his arms, clinging. "Oh, yes, my darling. I'll marry you."

With a groan of relief and joy, his lips found hers. Total commitment to their love was in the kiss. At length, he lifted his head and asked, "When?"

"I have to settle things with Harley first. I have to go to Gainesville," she said with sudden decision. "I have to sit down with the boys and Harley and get all the cards on the table. Whatever the outcome, I want to talk about it, face-to-face."

He kissed her again. "I'm so proud of you, Andy."

* * *

When Andy arrived at Harley's apartment in Gainesville, she was greeted by a small, dark-haired woman with huge brown eyes and bare feet, wearing shorts and a halter. "I hope I have the right apartment," Andy responded to the woman's questioning look. "Is this where Harley Darnell lives?" She hadn't warned Harley that she was coming, fearing he might take the boys somewhere else before she arrived.

"Yes."

"I'm Andrea Darnell, Harley's ex-wife."

The woman looked stunned, but she recovered quickly. "Oh! Well, come on in. Harley's gone down to Miami for a few days on business." Andy followed her into the small living room. The woman turned suddenly and offered Andy her hand. "I'm Donna. Donna Herbert. Brad and Tony have gone to a movie. They should be back in about an hour." She moved newspapers and magazines off a chair. "Sit down. Would you like something to drink? Tea? Coffee?"

Disappointed at not being able to see the boys immediately, Andy sat down. "No, thanks. I guess I should have let somebody know I was coming. I decided suddenly and, well, I thought it might be better..." Andy's voice trailed off.

Donna reached for a pack of cigarettes on the coffee table, lit one and, drawing on it, sat back in the couch. "You don't have to explain. Harley told me about his telephone conversation with you."

Andy shrugged, deciding to be honest. "I thought he might keep the boys away from me if he knew I was coming. He's been acting very unlike himself lately. I'm probably being paranoid, but this idea of Harley's to keep the boys with him has sort of knocked the props out from under me. We have to sit down, all four of us, and talk about it.''

Donna squinted at her through a cloud of smoke. ''May I speak frankly?''

''Please do.''

''I'm as shocked as you are by this sudden fatherly streak in Harley. He asked me to move out of the apartment while the boys were here, and I agreed. I figured the kids only had two weeks to spend with their dad, and they didn't need me around. Then this trip to Miami came up, and Harley asked me to move back in to be with the boys while he was gone.'' She leaned forward to tap her cigarette on the rim of a glass ashtray. ''That's when he told me about this insane notion of keeping Brad and Tony with him—with us.''

''Insane?'' Andy smiled. ''Then you're not exactly crazy about the idea?''

''Look, Andy—may I call you Andy?'' At Andy's nod, Donna went on, ''I'm a nurse—I'm on vacation now. I work the graveyard shift at a local hospital, and I sleep days. Harley has a steady job at the moment, selling electrical supplies, but he's already talking about looking for something else. We can get by on my salary—barely. But with two growing boys...'' She paused, as though to consider her words, before continuing. ''Brad and Tony are good kids, Andy, but I've never been around children. I never really wanted any of my own. Maybe I satisfy whatever maternal instinct I have caring for patients. The three of us have been alone here for two days and we're already starting to get on each others' nerves. To tell you the truth, that's why I sent them to a movie this afternoon—there's a theater just five blocks from here. Between you and me, I'm seriously considering moving out permanently if you let Harley keep the boys."

"Does Harley know this?"

"I didn't think I'd have to give him an ultimatum. I assumed you'd come after the kids."

"I hope that's the way it turns out," Andy said, liking the woman, although she had never expected to. "But Joe—Joe Underwood, my fiancé—convinced me I have to consider the boys' wishes, too."

"Joe. He's the guy that started all this." She laughed harshly and took another drag on her cigarette. "When the boys first got here, they talked about Joe all the time. Harley nearly blew a gasket. The kids shut up about Joe pretty quick." She eyed Andy narrowly. "Does Harley know you're going to marry the guy?"

Andy shook her head. "I've only known it a few days myself. Donna, Joe doesn't want to take Harley's place."

"You'd better tell Harley that."

"Will he listen to me?"

"He wouldn't have two weeks ago." Donna grinned suddenly. "To tell you the truth, I don't think Harley had to go to Miami just now. I think the constant togetherness with Brad and Tony, after living a bachelor life for so long, was starting to get to him. They were getting on his nerves. He felt awful about that, but—"

"It didn't stop him from going to Miami," Andy finished for her. As Joe had said, Harley hadn't undergone a character transformation.

Donna stubbed out her cigarette and leaned toward Andy. "You know what? If we handle this thing right, I'll bet we can get Harley to admit the boys are better off with you."

Andy understood what Donna was suggesting. They should soothe Harley's ruffled feathers, prop up his ego and let Harley feel magnanimous by allowing him to believe the ultimate decision was his alone. Donna was suggesting that they rescue Harley from another of his wrongheaded impulses by allowing him to save face. Well, Andy knew how to do that. She'd spent her married life doing it. Now it appeared that Donna had taken up where Andy had left off. For the first time, Andy felt sorry for the woman.

Later, the boys returned, saw Andy, yelped with delight and nearly knocked her off her feet when they ran into her arms. That was the moment when Andy began to believe that everything was going to be all right.

The flight to Omaha left at nine-thirty Saturday morning. Harley, in a jocular mood, drove them to the airport. He acted, Andy reflected, like a man who had just been released from jail. Donna, it turned out, had been absolutely right. After almost two weeks with the boys, Harley was having second thoughts about spending the next several years under the tight restraints of full-time fatherhood. He'd have died before he'd have admitted it, though.

Andy and the boys had made it easy for him. She had told Harley that she wanted to discuss the situation calmly, and that she was willing to let the boys make the final decision if he was. After spending two

days with the children, she was pretty sure they were
having second thoughts of their own, if indeed they
had ever really wanted to stay with Harley in the first
place.

It was Brad who had clinched it. He'd turned to his
father and said, "Dad, I've been thinking about living with you all the time. I know we'd have lots of fun,
like you said, and we'd get to go to the beach every
weekend and sail and dive. The trouble is I want to
stay with you, but I want to go with Mom, too. If I
stay here, I'd have to go to a new school and make new
friends. But I like the friends I have, and I'd miss
them. I'd miss Mom, too, and Grandpa, and, well, I
think I'd rather live with Mom, if it's all right with
you."

Watching Harley as Brad spoke, Andy hadn't
missed the gradual release of tension in his body.
Avoiding Andy's look, Harley had asked Tony, "Do
you feel the same way as Brad?"

Tony had ducked his head. "Yeah, Dad, I do."
He'd looked up with a sudden grin. "We could come
back and see you next summer, Dad."

Harley had cleared his throat and clapped his big
hands on his sons' backs. "Well, boys, you know I
only want what's best for you. To tell you the truth,
Andy, I'm afraid I'm going to have to change my
plans. With this new plastics deal I'm getting into, I'll
have to be on the road a lot. Maybe it's best if the boys
go back to Neptune with you for now. Yes, I definitely think that would be best."

Harley hadn't mentioned Joe, even though Donna
must have told him about Andy's wedding plans. But
because of Joe, Harley would undoubtedly be more

attentive to his sons in the future, Andy thought as they said goodbye to Harley and boarded the plane.

Once they were airborne, Brad said, "Mom, I never wanted to stay with Dad all the time, not really. I just didn't want to hurt his feelings."

"Me, too," Tony said, not to be outdone.

Sitting between them, Andy patted both their hands. "No explanations are needed, guys. We worked it out just fine."

"Is Joe going to meet our plane?" Tony asked.

"Yes. Is that all right with you?"

"Well, sure," Tony said. "We missed him, didn't we, Brad?"

"Yeah," Brad agreed with enthusiasm, "we sure did."

Andy smiled and settled back in her seat. The boys were obviously glad to be able to talk about Joe again. It must have been difficult for them to curb their enthusiasm when Harley was around. She wondered how long it would take for Harley's charm to wear thin with Donna. Perhaps it never would. Silently, she wished them luck.

Joe was waiting at the gate in the Omaha airport, with a big grin of welcome on his face. Heedless of anybody else, Andy walked straight into his arms. He hugged her fiercely, then drew away reluctantly to speak to the boys.

"Welcome home, you two."

"We're sure glad to be here," Tony said.

Brad had watched Joe and Andy's embrace carefully. He didn't seem to mind, Andy noted. "Seems like we've been gone two months instead of two weeks," he said. He turned to Andy, "Mom, can we get our luggage by ourselves?"

"Sure." Andy dug the claim tickets from her purse. "Here. Wait for us there. We'll be along in a few minutes."

As soon as they were out of sight, she threw her arms around Joe's neck and kissed him hungrily. "Mmmm, I've missed kissing you."

"God, I've missed you, too. You have enslaved me, woman. I'm not worth a damn without you, even for a few days."

She tilted her head back to look up at him. "I'm glad, because I thought I'd die before I got back here to you."

He kissed the tip of her nose. "Was it tough?"

"Not nearly as bad as I thought it would be." She proceeded to tell him briefly about what had happened in Florida.

"I'm glad Harley decided not to make trouble," he said when she'd finished. "The boys would have been the ones to suffer most. By the way, did you tell them about our plans?"

"I wanted us to do it together."

He gave her a lopsided smile. "Together. I like the sound of that. We'll do everything together from now on."

She stood on tiptoe to move her lips lightly over his. "With Pop right next door and a ready-made family, you might get more togetherness than you've bargained for."

"Impossible," he growled and crushed her mouth with his in a quick, yearning kiss.

When he released her, her cheeks were glowing. "I think we're making a spectacle of ourselves," she said breathlessly. "People are staring."

"They're jealous," he assured her as he threw an arm over her shoulders. "Come on, honey. Let's go home."

*　*　*　*　*

Silhouette Special Edition
COMING NEXT MONTH

AVAILABLE THIS MONTH:

Silhouette Romance™
Legendary Lovers Trilogy

BY DEBBIE MACOMBER....

ONCE UPON A TIME, in a land not so far away, there lived a girl, Debbie Macomber, who grew up dreaming of castles, white knights and princes on fiery steeds. Her family was an ordinary one with a mother and father and one wicked brother, who sold copies of her diary to all the boys in her junior high class.

One day, when Debbie was only nineteen, a handsome electrician drove by in a shiny black convertible. Now Debbie knew a prince when she saw one, and before long they lived in a two-bedroom cottage surrounded by a white picket fence.

As often happens when a damsel fair meets her prince charming, children followed, and soon the two-bedroom cottage became a four-bedroom castle. The kingdom flourished and prospered, and between soccer games and car pools, ballet classes and clarinet lessons, Debbie thought about love and enchantment and the magic of romance.

One day Debbie said, "What this country needs is a good fairy tale." She remembered how well her diary had sold and she dreamed again of castles, white knights and princes on fiery steeds. And so the stories of Cinderella, Beauty and the Beast, and Snow White were reborn....

Look for Debbie Macomber's *Legendary Lovers* trilogy from Silhouette Romance: *Cindy and the Prince* (January, 1988); *Some Kind of Wonderful* (March, 1988); *Almost Paradise* (May, 1988). Don't miss them!

SRT-1